LION ON THE
MOUNTAIN

LION ON THE MOUNTAIN

Paige Dixon

Illustrated by J. H. Breslow

ATHENEUM *1972* NEW YORK

for Bob

LION ON THE MOUNTAIN

1

IT WAS COOL IN THE LONG NARROW TACK ROOM THAT connected the barn with the house. Through the open door, Jamie could see the red sumac bushes across the yard, announcing autumn before most of the trees had gotten around to it. The chokecherry had turned, too; in the mountains, the aspen were gold, and the sky was that bright blue that you saw only in the fall. The paper said there was a foot of new snow on Long's Peak.

A field mouse scampered across the floor, and Daisy, the big orange and white cat, stretched out on a shelf above Jamie, blinked her green eyes, and twitched her tail once. The twitch whisked to the floor one of the turkey feathers that Jamie was using for fletching his arrows. He picked it up and tickled

3

Daisy's nose. "You're a lazy good-for-nothing monster," he said. It was the cock feather. The cock feather was the important one, Ted had taught him; when you held the arrow right, the cock feather had to be at right angles to the bowstring, so the feathers wouldn't give much resistance when you shot your arrow. And the little ridge in the nock at the end of the arrow would line up with the cock feather to guide you. Tongue between his teeth, Jamie carefully fitted the feather on the trimmer and burned and trimmed it the way he wanted it.

He tensed at the sound of steps in the yard behind him, expecting his father to come in with his critical comments. "What do you want to mess around with all that stuff for?" he would say. "Ted always told you there's no sense to making your own arrows when you can buy aluminum or fiberglass that are a whole lot better. Here you went and spent some of your paper route money on that dumb fletching rig and that feather trimmer last year, and what are they good for?"

And Jamie never had any answer for him. He knew the aluminum and fiberglass arrows would last a lot longer, and they were more accurate; they wouldn't warp, and they hardly ever broke. The only thing was, Jamie liked to make his own; he had never even tried to explain to his father. If Ted had

4

said it was stupid to make your own, then, for his father, it was stupid to make your own. You couldn't argue about it. He would probably have stopped listening before you finished telling him, anyway.

But the approaching footsteps didn't crunch on the gravel the way his father's boots did. He heard, instead, the soft slap of sneakered feet on the floor boards, and without turning, he said, "Hi, Cissy."

"Oh, you," his cousin Cissy said. "I was sneaking up on you, like an Indian maiden. How come you heard me?"

He laughed. "I hear like a mountain lion, see like an eagle, and smell like a fox."

She plopped down on the floor beside him. "You smell like a big baboon." She pulled a wad of Kleenex from the pocket of her torn cutoffs and blew her nose. "Not that I could tell."

"How's your hay fever?"

"Terrible. You know it's terrible; why do you ask such a dumb question? It's ragweed time."

He liked Cissy, and he was sorry she had hay fever. Her small nose was bright red, and her dark blue eyes watered from the middle of August till the first heavy frost. Cissy was nine, and the doctor said she might outgrow it. Meanwhile, she had weekly shots, took antihistamines, and sneezed.

"Are you getting ready to go hunting?"

5

"I guess so." He wished she hadn't brought it up. He liked to wander through the forest shooting his bow or Ted's crossbow, testing his accuracy, bringing down a particular pine cone or lopping the head off a spear of bear grass, but he didn't like to kill game. Since the terrible expense of Ted's medical bills, though, they were poor, worse than poor, and the family would have to have game to get them through the winter. His father hadn't mentioned going hunting, but he would soon. He had been cleaning his guns in the evenings. He was nearsighted, and even with his glasses, he was not nearly as good a hunter as Jamie was, or as Ted had been. He would need Jamie to bring home a deer, maybe an elk if they were lucky. No antelope this year, though. Last year, Ted had won a permit in the special drawing, and he had gotten his antelope, but this year, Jamie and Pa hadn't lucked out. They would have to get some pheasant and maybe some sage grouse to fill the locker.

"Papa says you're a better shot with the bow and arrow than anybody," Cissy said. She pushed a strand of hair out of her eyes. Her tan was beginning to fade already, and soon, the freckles that she despised so would begin to pale out.

When the sumac turns red, Jamie thought, and Cissy's freckles start to go, you know it's getting on toward winter. He finished the arrow and stretched languidly. He felt like going for a walk in the woods, but it was about time to feed the heifers and hogs and haul water for the horses. There was always something to do, and sometimes he felt like a chore machine. Get up at five and deliver the papers; grab a bite to eat and rush like mad for school; come home and do the evening chores; eat supper, do your homework, and fall into bed. On weekends, though, he had some time to himself, and Pa and Ma were good about not pestering him to account for himself. They probably knew he was just puttering around in the woods practicing with his bow or tracking some animal to get a shot with his Instamatic. Or more likely, they didn't give much thought to where he was. Not that they weren't good to him—when they thought about him. Ma fed him good and took care of his clothes and sometimes reminded him to go to the dentist or something. But their minds were still on Ted. They always had been. Ted, five years older than Jamie, had been the perfect son. Did everything right. Eagle Scout when he was a kid, liked everybody, everybody liked him, made the ski team his first year at the university, and skiied in Europe with the American team the second year. Got good grades. Great hunter, great mountain climber, great everything—you name it, man, and

Ted was the best. It was a tough act to follow.

And it had become even tougher when Ted died. He'd gone climbing up Long's Peak in late October with a couple of fraternity brothers. Long's Peak was a rugged climb, but Ted had made it a half-dozen times before. This time, they had gotten caught in a blizzard when they were more than half-way down, and Ted, probably blinded by the snow, had fallen into a narrow ravine. He was still alive when they found him, but he had never regained consciousness.

As far as Jamie was concerned, Ted had died on the mountain. The thin white mask of a face, the shaved head, the body lying inert under the hos-pital sheet, bottles and tubes attached to its arms, Jamie did not recognize as his brother. But Ted had existed like that until April. Every day his parents had gone to see him, and several times a week Jamie went, too, trying not to look, trying to keep his gaze fixed on the big willow tree across the street. Ted would have hated having them see him like that; it seemed indecent to look. His mother still cried a lot, silently and by herself; her eyes were always swol-len, and she never talked much any more. His father tried to be hearty, to cheer her up, but it didn't work, and sooner or later he, too, would subside into gloomy silence, pretending to read the paper or rushing outside to do some chore that had already been done. It seemed even worse lately.

"Hey, there's one missing." Cissy was standing in front of the bow and arrow rack that hung on the wall, counting the arrows. She always counted the arrows when she came over.

"Naturally. This one. I'm working on it."

"Oh, yeah." She rubbed the back of her sun-burned mosquito-bitten leg with the other foot. "I wish you'd teach me to shoot a bow."

"Someday I will."

"You always say that."

"I really will." He looked at her, wondering if she, too, felt that nobody paid any attention to her. She was the youngest in a family of six, and she had had to learn to fend for herself. "Honest, I will, Cis. We'll have to get you a smaller bow, though."

"Okay." Satisfied, she sat down on the worn leather sofa that Ted had bought at the Good Will. A lot of Ted's gear still hung on the walls: his saddles, skis, ski boots, snowshoes, some of his guns, and the crossbow. But right after his death, all his mountain-climbing gear disappeared—ropes, boots, pitons, everything. Jamie assumed that his father had gotten rid of it, perhaps at his mother's request. It was a shame, in a way, because Ted had spent a lot of money on that gear. But maybe somebody was enjoying it. Climbing didn't interest Jamie, except when it was necessary to stalk game or get some spectacular pictures.

Now he did hear his father's boots crack and crunch on the gravel. He'd been out in the south pasture mending fence. Jamie had helped him for a while, until his father said, impatiently, that he could do it faster himself. Jamie was glad; he hated the tedious job. But to make up for his inadequacy, hoping to please his father, he had milked the new Jersey cow. They'd gotten her yesterday from Seth Anderson, and she was a pretty little thing. It was the first milk cow they'd had since old Bessie died, and Jamie was glad to have the fresh milk and good rich cream again. Sometimes, they bought it from the Andersons, but it wasn't like having your own.

His father's tall thin shadow cut across the floor of the tack room.

"Hi, Uncle Clarke," Cissy said. She went over and gave her uncle a quick hug.

He smiled down at her indulgently. "How are you, Cissy?"

"Great. Except for my stupid nose." She sneezed as if on signal.

"You ought not to hang around here—too much hay for you."

"I know it. But it's so bad anyway, it doesn't make

a heck of a lot of difference."

Jamie's father came further into the room, glanced with a slight frown at the fletching rig, but, to Jamie's relief, said nothing about it. Snow, the wire-haired terrier, trotted in and sat down on Jamie's feet, waiting to have his ears scratched.

"I milked the cow," Jamie said. "She gives a lot of good milk. She's a real good cow." Sometimes, in the face of his father's silence, he found himself talking too much, chattering like a girl.

"You better leave her to me," his father said. "Seth says she's got a bit of a temper."

"She was fine."

"Better leave her to me."

Jamie sighed. He was sixteen; he was just two inches short of his father's six feet, and he outweighed him by fifteen pounds. He'd grown up on farms and worked with animals all his life. When was his father going to decide that he was old enough to be treated like a man? He couldn't remember Ted's ever having been spoken to as if he were a clumsy boy, incompetent. Nobody, for instance, had ever called him Teddy. Jamie longed for his father to call him Jim. Silently, he put away the fletching rig and fitted the arrow into the rack. In a minute, his father would remind him to feed the hogs and fill the horses' watering trough, although he had been doing these things for years and had never forgotten.

His father reached his long arms up and took down the .32 Winchester special. "Tell your papa," he said to Cissy, "I plan to bring him some meat this weekend."

"You going hunting already, Uncle Clarke?" Cissy glanced at Jamie.

He could have told me, Jamie thought. He must have been planning it.

"You and Jamie going hunting?" Cissy said again.

"Yep. Day after tomorrow, the good Lord willin', and the crick don't rise." He winked at her. "Bring you some tasty venison."

Cissy blew her nose. "You better let Jamie take his bow, Uncle Clark."

"How's that, Cis?"

"Because you know how good he is. He can shoot clean and quick, and the deer won't suffer much."

"Well, I guess he can take his bow if he's got a mind to. You want to hunt with your bow, Jamie?"

"Yes, if I'm goint to hunt."

His father's mouth tightened slightly. "You're going to hunt, boy. We need meat." He turned to Cissy. "So you don't think your old uncle's much of a shot, do you?"

"Well, you're all right, Uncle Clarke, but you *are*

near-sighted, and I worry about the deer."

"Cissy, the Sangre de Cristos are full of deer. There are so many of 'em, they'd starve to death over the winter if hunters didn't take out some of them."

His father said this every year. It was true, of course, but it always seemed to him his father really didn't like to kill them either and was looking for an excuse. He hated the out-of-town hunters who came in and killed for the fun of it, often leaving wounded animals, sometimes wounding or killing each other. "City assassins," he called them. It was one of the few things Jamie and his father agreed on.

"I saw a mountain lion the other day," Jamie said. "If people would leave them alone, they'd help keep down the herd."

His father looked at him sharply. "Hadn't heard about any lions up there for some time. Where'd you see it?"

Jamie described as well as he could the brushy draw far up in the hills where he had first seen sign, and later, had noticed that a mountain lion was trailing him.

"Wow!" Cissy said. "Weren't you scared?"

He laughed. It was nice to have caught not only Cissy's attention but his father's. "Nah. He was just curious. They won't jump you. That's a myth. I could just barely see him every once in a while, when the sun hit him. He was big."

"How big?" his father said.

"Oh, I don't know. Maybe a hundred fifty pounds. I couldn't see him long enough to tell for sure. His tracks were about four inches.

"He's probably long gone by now," his father said.

"Well, you know how they are. They'll go up to sixty or seventy miles, but they usually circle back." He wondered why his father was asking him about the lion. He knew as much about them as Jamie did, at least as far as facts went. Pa wasn't much of a tracker anymore, though. Jamie was better. He was even better at it than Ted—Ted had told him so himself—he was more patient. A few years ago, Ted had bought Snow from a man in Arizona who had trained him to hunt lions. They'd tracked one to its den, a mother with two kits still with their spots on. Since he'd seen the big one the other day, Jamie had been meaning to take Snow and track it. If he could get a good picture, he could sell it to one of the hunting magazines and surprise his father with the check. His father worried about money all the time because they still owed the hospital and the doctors thousands of dollars.

His father rumpled Cissy's tangled hair. "You'd

better get on home, young 'un. It's getting on toward supper time."

"Okay," she said. She picked up Snow and hugged him. The dog rolled his small dark eyes and gave Cissy a quick lick of his tongue on her ear. Then he struggled to get down. "All right, Snow, if you want to be ornery. I was just trying to show you I loved you."

Jamie's father laughed. "You were squeezing him to death." He took the .32 and opened the door to the kitchen. "Tell your ma to get out her venison recipes, Cis. Jamie, don't forget the hogs."

Jamie could smell something good from the kitchen. Apple pie, it smelled like. That was a good sign, if his mother felt up to making pie. The door closed behind his father. "I got to finish the chores," he said to Cissy.

She sneezed and mopped her eyes with a limp Kleenex. "All right, I'm going. If you find any pretty feathers, bring them home. I'm collecting them." At the door, she gave him a quick sideways look. "You take care, when you go hunting—you hear me?"

"I always take care."

"Mama says you're worth your weight in gold, but I told her gold's not as valuable as it used to be." She gave him a teasing smile and ran off down the avenue to the county road. Just before she disappeared over the first rise, she waved without looking back, as if she knew he was watching her.

He laughed and shook his head. That Cissy. But he felt very good about Aunt Martha's saying that about him. Whistling, he went to feed the pigs.

2

JAMIE ROLLED OVER SLEEPILY AND SHUT OFF HIS alarm. It was three a.m. A lot of people all over the world are just going to bed now, he thought. He yawned, forced himself to sit up, and swung his feet onto the cold floor. He could hear his mother in the kitchen, and he could smell bacon and coffee.

He and his father had packed the night before, so there wasn't much left to do. After he brushed his teeth, he stuck the toothbrush into his back pack and closed it. He wore jeans under a pair of heavier hunting pants. They were going to take the horses up into the mountains, and you never knew whether you were going to be hot or cold—probably both. He pulled his old sweat shirt over his head and took out of the closet the reversible down-filled hunting jacket that his aunt and uncle had given him last Christmas. He turned it to the red side. It was a neat jacket, the best jacket he'd ever had.

On his way to the stairs, he glanced into Ted's room. His mother had not let anyone change anything in the room since the accident. Ted's light nylon jacket hung on the back of the chair at his desk. His Wellington boots were lined up neatly, as he had left them, at the foot of the bed. Even the handful of change he'd taken from his pocket—systematically stacked in dimes, nickels, and quarters—was on the bureau. Jamie shivered. He wished his mother would let them do something about that room. It seemed morbid to leave it as if Ted might come in any minute. You had to face it, he was gone.

In the kitchen, his father was already eating breakfast, and his mother was frying more bacon. She gave him her quick sad little smile. "Good morning, dear."

"Morning, Ma." He thought she looked a little better than she sometimes did, as if she might have gotten some sleep for a change. Both his parents were in their fifties, and since Ted's accident, they looked much older, especially his mother.

He got the pack of emergency rations he always carried when he went into the woods—a chunk of jerky, some boxes of raisins, a couple of candy bars

—and put it in the big inner pocket of his jacket. He checked to make sure he had his camera and film, Ted's good binoculars, and the hunting knife in a sheath attached to his belt. He glanced out the window at the horse trailer that his father had already hitched up to the pickup.

He looked at his father. "Four horses? Do we need two packhorses, just for a few days?"

His father took a long swallow of coffee before he answered. "We're going to have company."

"Company?"

"Yeah. We're going to meet a fellow out at the fork who wants to go with us."

Jamie was puzzled. "Who is it?"

His father shrugged, wiped his mouth, got up from the table. "A guy from Denver, name of Darby French."

Jamie knew his father didn't like to be cross-examined, but he wanted to understand what was going on. "Who is he?"

"He's a guy who wants to go hunting," his father said impatiently.

"He's a cousin of Seth Anderson's," his mother told him. "Sit down and eat, dear."

Jamie sat down. He didn't like the idea of a stranger going with them. And he couldn't understand why his father hadn't mentioned it. "Is he a city assassin?" He tried to make it sound like a joke, but they both knew it wasn't.

"He is a man," his father said, emphasizing his words the way he did when he meant to be sarcastic, "he is a man who wants to go hunting, and he will pay—quite well, as a matter of fact—for somebody to take him. In case you've forgotten, I happen to be in need of money." He put his cup and saucer in the sink and stalked out of the room.

Jamie looked down at the worn linoleum that was pockmarked with boot-heel marks. "He just took me by surprise," he said.

His mother sat down in the chair his father had left. Her face was pale and drawn. "Your father worries about the money we owe."

"I know that. If he'd only let me drop out of school, I could help . . ."

"You're not dropping out of school." She spoke with unusual sharpness. "We haven't sunk that low. You're finishing high school, and you're going to college, and there's no argument about it."

Jamie shrugged. You couldn't win for losing. He felt like a big jerk, living off them when they were having such a hard time. He gave them his paper route money, but it didn't amount to much. The way he figured it, he could drop out of school and get a job with Fish and Game. He'd already talked to his friend Stan over there. He could always go back and finish later when things were better. But you couldn't talk to them. They cut him off short, just the way they'd always done. To them, he was a little boy, and they didn't have to consult him or listen to his side of things.

He finished his breakfast hurriedly and jumped up as he heard his father rev the engine on the pickup. He grabbed his pack and his jacket and kissed his mother on the cheek. "Go over to Aunt Martha's for supper, okay?" He didn't like to think of her being alone.

She turned away. "I'll see." When he reached the door, she said, "Be careful, Jamie."

"Sure. You know me. Old Man Caution." He pushed the door open with his foot and went out to the pickup. He had stacked his archery equipment and his bedroll in the back of the pickup the night before. He tossed in his pack and got in beside his father.

Snow ran up to the door and tried to jump in.

"No, Snow," Jamie said. He started to close the door.

"Let him come."

Jamie stared at his father. "*Deer* hunting?"

"He knows how to behave. Let him come along."

Jamie opened the door, and Snow leaped into his

lap. Pa's got something on his mind, Jamie thought. He's up to something. Then, as the truck started down the avenue, wheels crunching on the frost-covered gravel, he saw his father glance back at the house, up at Ted's room, and he thought he understood. Pa was thinking about last year, hunting with Ted. Ted had taken Snow along because he had had it in his mind that they might pick up the trail of a mountain lion. But what would Pa want with a mountain lion? He was strictly a businesslike hunter; he wanted meat, not trophies. Huddling into the snug warmth of his jacket and pulling Snow up against his chest, Jamie decided his father was feeling lonesome for Ted—that was why he took Snow.

As they came out onto the road, Jamie looked back at the house. He couldn't see the kitchen light from there; the house looked bleak in the darkness, not shadowy the way things sometimes look in the dark, but solid and a little threatening. He shivered. If I were going to do anything kooky about Ted, the way Ma does, he thought, what I'd do is, I'd leave a light burning in his room, day and night. But that was a crazy idea. He could imagine Pa's reaction to that one—Pa, who went around turning off lights all the time.

He glanced at Pa's profile, thin, angular, stern except when he smiled. Pa liked maxims, and when you looked at his face, you could almost see him thinking, "Onward and upward; the race is to the swift; to thine own self be true." Well, Pa had had a hard life; you had to have something to hang onto. Anyway, that was what Ted had said.

When they passed Cissy's house, a light went on in her bedroom. Jamie leaned over to toot the horn, but his father raised his arm to block him.

"No sense waking up the whole bunch."

Jamie was sorry he couldn't signal Cissy. Poor old Ciss, she didn't sleep well in hay fever season. He hoped he could find her some good feathers.

Pa reached over and flipped on the heater, and Jamie felt the welcome warmth come in around his knees. It was really cold at this time of day.

They went by the Anderson place. There was a light in the big farmhouse and lights in the barn. Pa slowed down and turned left toward the fork. They didn't usually go this way. Then Jamie remembered the stranger, who, for a few minutes, he had forgotten. What would he be like? He knew if he asked, his father would say, "Hold on a minute and find out for yourself."

The truck eased to a stop, and Jamie could see the dark outline of a man standing by the road. The man waved and came toward the truck, bringing his gear and his gun. Probably some city dude. Anybody that had to pay somebody to take him hunting . . . Well, he and Pa could hunt together, and Jamie could take off by himself, he hoped. He hoped Pa didn't have drive hunting in mind. Jamie hated that—several guys, sometimes a whole big bunch, closing in on one deer. It seemed unsporting. Jamie preferred stalking, if he had to hunt at all. That way, it was just him and the deer, and they each had an even chance to win.

The man outside opened the door and said, "Good morning!"

Jamie couldn't see him too clearly, but he saw that he was not a very big man—maybe five-foot-eight or so, and thin. He had a small trimmed beard and long sideburns, and when he smiled, white even teeth. I was right, Jamie thought, a dude.

" 'Morning!" Pa leaned past Jamie. "Hop in. You can throw your gear in the back. Jamie, you and Snow move over."

Jamie heard the thump of the man's pack, which was very big, and he mentally crossed his fingers, hoping it hadn't landed on his arrows.

Laughing, the man climbed in, slammed the door, and said, "Wow! It's cold!" He took off his leather gloves and rubbed his fingers.

"Yep," Pa said. "Winter's on her way."

The man laughed again. " 'If winter comes, can spring be far behind?' "

Jamie had heard the line, somewhere along the way, in an English class. It didn't strike him as being very appropriate.

"This is my boy Jamie," Pa said.

"Hi, Jamie." The man turned his dazzling white smile on Jamie. "I'm Darby French. What's your dog's name?"

"Snow," Jamie said.

"I'll be darned. Well, he is kind of snowy looking, isn't he? Or maybe more like popcorn. Did you name him?"

"No, my brother did. Snow was his dog."

"Oh, I see."

He could tell that the man didn't see at all, that he didn't know about Ted. Well, it was none of his business.

"How was the weather up in Denver?" Pa asked.

Jamie had never heard Pa make idle conversation. This guy must be paying a lot of money to go hunting.

"Oh, yesterday was warm—and smoggy. It's gotten so you get up in the morning and you can't see the mountains anymore."

Pa made a clucking sound. "Terrible. I don't know what's going to come of it all."

"Or why we put up with it," Darby French said. "That's the real puzzle. We're always bragging about what an adaptable animal man is; well, if you ask me, we're adapting ourselves right out of existence. Smog, traffic, taxes, ghettos, overcrowding—we put up with it all. That's why I like to get back to nature whenever I can." Darby pulled a pipe and and oilskin tobacco pouch out of his pocket and began to tamp tobacco into the bowl of the pipe. He didn't have much room to do it, and some of the tobacco fell to the floor. "I grew up in the country. New Hampshire."

"Nice country, is it?" Pa said.

"Used to be. Now it's touristed to death."

A faint light was showing in the sky behind the mountains. It would be a while yet, though, before the sun got up over the peaks. Jamie could just barely make out the pale glimmer of the snow that covered them. If the sun were up, they would be able to see the glacier, pink and granular, off to the north.

Pa pulled off the highway onto a narrow dirt road leading to the deserted mine where they always left the pickup. From there, they would go on up into the mountains on horseback, and finally they would leave the horses and hunt on foot.

Pa eased the pickup carefully down the rutted

road, glancing into the rear-view mirror to make sure the horse trailer was all right. "Seth tells me you're a teacher," he said to Darby.

Darby shrugged. "Yeah. A real he-man profession." He sounded scornful.

"We sure need good teachers."

"It's a woman's job."

"I don't know about that. I think kids need a man's hand, too. What do you teach?"

"English."

"High school?" Jamie asked.

"No, junior college. It's no better."

Jamie felt vaguely uneasy. "Why do you do it, if you don't like it?"

"Oh, a guy gets trapped. It sounded great when I was in college. I saw myself in a big university. I'd hold small seminars in my study, I thought—me in my big leather chair with my pipe—and we'd explore ideas." He gave a bitter laugh. "It didn't turn out quite that way. But I've got an expensive wife and three kids to support."

"It's hard to do a job you don't like," Pa said, and it occurred to Jamie that Pa probably never had. He'd done a lot of things in his life—logging, tuna fishing, rodeo riding, the Navy—but he talked about them as if they'd all been pretty exciting. Jamie felt a stirring of pride in his father; he was darned sure nobody had ever pushed Pa into a stupid job or could keep him there if they did.

"It's hell," Darby said gloomily.

"My boy, my other boy, was studying business administration up at the university."

"Smart boy," Darby grunted. Pa just nodded, and everyone was quiet, talked out already.

The pickup turned off the narrow road onto a trail that most people wouldn't even have noticed. And in a few minutes, the dark low shadow of the mine portal came into sight. Pa stopped the truck and said, "Here we are."

Jamie helped him unload and pack the horses while Darby stood watching them. They fitted panniers on their mounts and packed the rest of the gear on the two packhorses, working with the speed and efficiency of long experience.

"I'd offer to help," Darby said, "but I'm no great hand with a horse."

"That's all right. We've got it." Pa led Gypsy forward and handed the lines to Darby. "She's a good steady little mare. Not so young anymore, but she's smart and careful."

Darby laughed. "You've got me pegged, Mr. Reed, when it comes to horses."

"Better call me Clarke," Pa said. "We're going to get to know each other real well in the next couple days." He held Gypsy while Darby climbed clumsily into the saddle. He handed Darby his gun. "That looks like Seth's .30–.30."

"It is. I bought myself a really good small-caliber rifle, but Seth wouldn't let me bring it. He said it wasn't a sporting gun. I don't know what he meant; the guy in the store said it was a fine gun. But you know, you don't argue with Seth."

Pa mounted his gelding with the long-legged ease that Jamie always envied. "Well, I guess you might say, the most sporting gun is the one that kills the game quickest. Those high-velocity jobs are apt to just wound an animal."

"Now why couldn't Seth have told me that," Darby said. "That makes sense."

Pa moved his horse into the lead position, and Jamie brought up the rear on his little buckskin mare, Candy, behind the two packhorses. "We'll take 'er slow till it gets a little lighter," Pa said. "Barring anything surprising, you'll find Gypsy is steady as she goes. She's been around here a good many times." He clucked to his horse and started off along the edge of a small creek, the water shallow and moving sluggishly now along the bed, its spring and early summer rush long gone.

Jamie half-dozed in the saddle. In his more wakeful moments, he thought about Darby. He disliked

everything about him, but he knew that wasn't fair. The man was trying to be friendly. Jamie tried to think what it would be like to be in Darby's shoes, but it was beyond his powers of imagination. He just could not understand people who let life trap them that way. Maybe he'd find out differently when he was older, but he didn't really think he would.

Near daybreak, the birds in the forest began chattering and singing and carrying on as if it were the first day of creation. Chipmunks and squirrels dashed from tree to tree. A badger waddled into the path right behind Candy's hoofs, and Snow barked at it. The forest was as noisy as Larimer Street on a Saturday night. Jamie had never been to Larimer Street that he knew of, though he had been to Denver several times, but that was an expression Ted had liked to use.

The air was still sharp, and he pulled up the hood of his jacket to keep the back of his neck warm. He noticed Darby's elegant saddle pants and boots. What a dude! He hoped he knew something about shooting so he wouldn't kill them off or wound any deer. People who wounded game and then didn't or couldn't find them made Jamie madder than almost anything. He had noticed that Darby had a good Bausch and Lomb scope on Seth's rifle; that ought to help. Pa never used a scope, but Ted had used one, and he always said Pa ought to. Ted had given Jamie a Bushnell 1.3X scope for his bow Christmas before last, but Jamie had never used it. He understood the reasoning about scopes, but somehow they didn't seem fair. But for someone like Darby, who probably could not hit the side of a barn door, yes.

Candy stumbled, and Jamie's binoculars and camera that hung around his neck smacked him in the ribs. He checked to make sure his bow hadn't shifted. Snow trotted along quietly beside Jamie, occasionally angling off to investigate an interesting smell.

They came out of the woods and moved up a narrow gorge. The light was beginning to filter in, and from time to time, Pa stopped to check on the signs. Jamie could see a fresh deer sign. Run, deer, he thought, and immediately felt guilty.

Pa stopped at their old camping site in a little valley, where they would leave the horses. From there on, the going was too rough for them. There was a lean-to in the valley that Pa and Ted had built several years ago, and that some of their friends used, too. It was always kept stocked with a few cans of beans and things in case of need. A grassy clearing near the lean-to made good grazing for the horses.

Pa and Jamie unloaded the gear, working fast because it was getting lighter all the time, and Pa wanted to get out hunting while the deer were still feeding. Darby tried to help, but he kept getting in their way, and finally, he stopped trying, busying himself with rearranging his own pack. While Jamie hobbled the horses, Pa got a little fire going for a pot of coffee. They drank it very hot, standing up, eating the cold bacon and egg sandwiches Ma had wrapped in waxed paper. Then Pa tied up Snow on a long rope. "Stay, boy. We'll see you later." He gave the dog half a sandwich.

"Sorry to hurry you," Pa said to Darby, "but we can eat later." He rinsed his cup with a slosh of water from the creek and hung the cup on his pack. "We'll be plenty hungry after we get those deer."

"You sound confident," Darby said.

Pa shrugged. "Lots of deer in here. Can't hardly miss." He put the water canteen and another package of sandwiches in the small shoulder pack he wore. Jamie strapped on his own pack.

"Here's how we'll work it," Pa said. He stepped out to the rim of the valley and scanned the timber line above him with his binoculars. He looked at Jamie and pointed toward an open place on a craggy slope. Jamie adjusted his glasses. Yes, they were there. Mule deer. Three that he could see. Chunky rugged bucks.

Pa handed the glasses to Darby with a grin. "One

apiece, for starters."

Darby fiddled with the glasses and finally got them right. "Wow!" he said. "Big guys. Hey, I can see their antlers!"

"Are you picturing those on your wall?" Pa sounded dry, and for a moment Jamie thought, He doesn't like Darby any better than I do; but then, he couldn't picture Pa going hunting with somebody who wasn't all right.

Darby laughed excitedly. "I wouldn't mind one goddamn bit." He gave the glasses back to Pa. "Let's go!"

"Here's how we'll work it," Pa said again. "The boy likes to stalk by himself. Jamie, you work the other side of that stand of pine . . ." He pointed away from the slope where the deer were. "See what you can pick up. Darby, you and me'll work together, about a hundred yards apart, till we get up to that creek . . ."

"What creek?" Darby said.

"Well, it's there. You'll see it. Then, I'll post you there, and I'll work around and drive 'em down toward you." He pulled his wool cap down over his forehead. "Mind you, don't pick me off by mistake."

Jamie looked quickly at Darby to see if he would take offense. Pa would never say such a thing to an experienced hunter.

But Darby, jiggling impatiently, said, "Don't worry. I'm after those antlers."

Pa glanced at Jamie. "Move on out."

Jamie took off fast, relieved at not having to be a part of that team. In a few seconds, he was out of sight of them. He knew this country as well as he knew his own bedroom. He found the little creek that rushed white and foaming down from the mountain and smoothed out in the meadow by the campsite. He followed it as far as the narrow canyon where Ted had gotten his big buck a year ago. There, he stopped and looked around. He could tell by the browse that the deer were still using the ground. There was about an inch of snow, which was good for stalking because he could move more quietly. He checked the quiver that hung from his belt and pulled his deerskin bowhunter gloves out of his pocket. It was still cold up in the hills, and his fingers felt stiff. He flexed them before he pulled on the gloves.

He stood still, trying to think like a deer, as Ted had taught him. Ahead of him, at the end of the canyon, the ground rose sharply and then leveled off again in thick brush. There could be half a dozen in there, he thought, and he'd never see them. As a rule, though, mule deer liked fairly open country. His father said they could see better than whitetail and blacktail, but Jamie didn't know how anyone would know that. Jamie swept the ground above him with his binoculars. He thought he saw a movement far up on the mountain, but he wasn't sure. He leaned against a tree to steady himself as he peered through the glasses. A spruce grouse whirred up into the air almost at his feet, and he laughed silently. A great hunter! He hadn't even seen the bird.

He moved forward slowly and quietly up to the end of the canyon. Catching hold of brush, he pulled himself up the steep side onto level ground. In the sharp clear air, he could smell pine and fern. He breathed in deeply, glad to be alive.

He skirted an open meadow, keeping just inside the trees. Suddenly, a doe leaped from a clump of laurel into the open area, crossing it in long high jumps, all four feet leaving the ground at once. She was impossible to shoot. He watched her graceful flight, glad he couldn't get her. In moments, she was out of sight on the other side of the clearing. She was probably looking back at him, though, Jamie thought; he lifted his hand in a wave. It was a good thing Pa couldn't see him—"my son who waves at deer."

Well, if there was that one, there were probably more around. He moved forward, climbing a little, going very slowly. Once, his bow caught on a sarvis berry bush, and he had to stop to loosen it. The snap of the branch would have alerted any deer that were nearby.

He climbed and circled for almost an hour, pausing often just to wait and see. You had to be patient in this business. He had been climbing gradually, but now he decided to get himself up on a rock ledge that looked like a good vantage point. He felt for handholds in the rocky outcropping. He caught hold of a bush, tested it, and decided it would do. He took off his gloves and put them in his pocket to avoid tearing them on the sharp edges of rock. He shifted his bow so it wouldn't catch and wrapped the fingers of one hand tightly around the bush. With the other hand, he found a shallow indentation in the rock. It would only take a couple of good thrusts up, and he'd have it made. He held his breath and took the first lunge up. This left him clinging to rock face, but it wasn't a terribly long drop if he missed. And he didn't intend to miss.

He squinted at the ledge above him. The sun was up now, and the rocks shone in the pale light, wet from melting snow. And wet meant slippery. He stood on tiptoe to reach for a small outcrop at the top of the ledge. He strained until he got his fingers around it, and then, with a heave that wrenched his shoulders, he went up, "walking" his boots fast up the slippery rock. He reached the top and fell forward onto a carpet of pine needles.

As soon as he got his breath, he sat up and looked around. He was in a perfect place, protected by a stand of Engelmann spruce about seventy feet tall. Below him, he could see the meadow where he had scared up the doe, and below that, the wooded area where the campsite was. And far away, just turning gold in the morning sun, a wide stretch of wild oats with the black strip of the road cutting through it. He pulled a candy bar from his pack and ate it, all the time watching the scene immediately below him. There was a bare grassy slope not far down, and he especially kept his eyes on that.

He leaned back against the purplish bark of the nearest spruce and waited. One reason he was a patient hunter, he thought, was that he would rather be in a place like the one he was in than anywhere else on earth. He could sit there forever.

Over his head, a goshawk floated lazily in the current of air, looking for his breakfast. Then below him, in a wild leap from cover, two bucks broke out and flew through the long grass. In seconds, he had an arrow fitted to his bow, but it was too late; they were gone again. He leaned forward, wondering what had spooked them. He was upwind of them and above them; he was sure they would not have caught his scent. And he had been very still. He leaned out a little further. Directly below him, another smaller ledge jutted out about halfway between him and the grassy slope. At first, he saw nothing, but then he caught his breath. A long tawny figure was stretched out on the edge, looking down. It was the mountain lion. Or anyway, *a* mountain lion, and he felt somehow sure it was the one he had seen the other day. He sat perfectly still, although the muscles in his back ached in his bent position. The lion was looking down at the slope, and twice his tail twitched, like old Daisy getting ready to jump a mouse. But there were no deer in sight that Jamie could see. Very cautiously, he lifted his binoculars and studied the lion. He *was* big! And beautiful. Jamie wished Ted could see him. He moved ever so slightly, trying to get his camera loose for a shot, but the movement dislodged a few tiny pebbles. They sprayed over the edge like water, and almost before Jamie could see him move, the lion was gone. And Jamie was staring down at an empty ledge through the finder of his camera.

3

DISAPPOINTED, HE SAT STILL FOR A MOMENT, WANT-ing to follow the big cat. But he was there to get deer meat, not to take pictures of a mountain lion. Pa would be awfully mad if he took off, and it might be days, if ever, before he could catch up with the cat. But anyway, he had seen him, and that was something.

One of the things the cat would surely have done was to scare off the deer. No hunting nearby for the time being. Jamie let himself down off the ledge, trying not to be in too big a hurry. Then he cut around to the smaller ledge where the cat had been. He stood on it himself, thinking, "He was here! Right here where I'm standing!" He tried to remember the exact color of the cat, maybe the color of fool's gold in the creek bed? No, he thought, darker than that, tawnier. He hadn't gotten a good look at the cat's face, but he knew most cats were dark around the eyes and the upper part of the muzzle with the lower flanks and belly almost white. He'd seen the white as the cat jumped; at least, he thought he had. It was hard to remember exactly what he had seen. He tried to find some disturbance in the dust on the ledge that would show the outline of the cat's body, but the rock showed nothing. Below him, though, where he'd jumped, there'd be prints.

Jamie bit off a piece of jerky and chewed on it, thinking. He had to get down to that little meadow anyway and find himself another hunting ground, so it wouldn't hurt to stop and look at the prints. After all, it would tell him which way the cat had gone, and that would be the way not to go if he wanted to find deer.

The sun was well up, and feeling the pleasant warmth on his shoulders, he unbuttoned the neck button of his parka and pulled the zipper part-way down. Far away, from the eastern side of the mountain as near as he could tell, he heard the high thin bugling of an elk. It always seemed funny that that was the best such a huge animal could do in the way of a mating call. With that chest, you'd expect something impressive.

"You better get lost, elk," he said aloud. "Mountain lion's out." Although he'd never heard of a mountain lion taking on an elk. Sometimes they went after livestock, and the ranchers got up in arms, but it had been a long time since Jamie had heard anything about that. As long as there were plenty of deer, the cat would be too smart to take chances with domestic animals. Cats were darned smart.

He swallowed his jerky and got to his knees, scanning the valley and the surrounding hills through his glasses. He'd better get cracking, or it would be too late to find a deer, and Pa would be disgusted with him. He wondered how they were doing. He hadn't heard any shots.

He climbed down the face of the cliff to the meadow, hampered by all his equipment, wishing he were a mountain lion and could make it in one graceful jump. Ted had told him a story he'd heard about a mountain lion killing a yearling calf and carrying it three miles up a mountain that was too steep for a man to climb.

He knelt down and examined the tracks in the damp ground. They were big, all right. With his finger, he traced the four toes and the dewclaw of the front feet. The cat's claws didn't show; they were retractable, like Daisy's. The marks of the hind feet weren't as distinct, but he could see that the hind paws were a little more elongated and had only four toes. He wondered if the designers of airplanes got the idea for retractable landing gears from cats.

Sighing, he stood up. Deer. He had to find himself a deer. Reluctantly, he set off in the opposite direction from the cat.

He walked for a long time over uneven ground: down into a gulley, then splashing through a shallow stream, then climbing. He began to see signs of deer browse again. He slowed down, keeping close to cover. Finally, he was up high once more, on the edge of an alpine meadow. Below him, the aspen made gold patterns among the conifers, and off to the south, far below, he could see a field of dark green winter wheat. Jamie sat down on a broad rock to catch his breath. He thought he heard a shot, way off to the west, but he wasn't sure. If it was, he hoped it was okay. He didn't trust Darby. Of course, there were probably other hunters in the mountains, too, though he hadn't seen any.

He hoped none of them would see the mountain lion. You weren't supposed to hunt mountain lions except in the spring, but hunters didn't always do what they were supposed to. Take care, big cat, he thought, keep out of sight. He'd come back another day with Snow and track the lion. Poor old Snow, sitting on a leash at the campsite. Jamie wondered again why his father had brought him.

A slight crackle of twigs off to his left brought Jamie's hand to the quiver of arrows. He pulled one quickly, moving as little as possible. He stared in the direction of the sound. A trickle of water coming down from a cirque in the rocks made a fast shallow stream when it got to the meadow, and out of the brush near the stream Jamie saw a reddish-tan muzzle appear. He fitted the arrow to the bow and waited. As the animal stepped into the clearing, Jamie relaxed. It was a pronghorn, a small beautiful buck with a fine set of forked horns. They didn't usually come up so high. Jamie sat without moving, watching the buck as it nervously scanned the country-side and then bent its head to drink, lifting it up anxiously every couple of seconds. He was glad he didn't have an antelope permit.

Suddenly, startled by something, the pronghorn leaped sideways and took off at tremendous speed down toward a lower meadow. Jamie remembered hearing that they could travel seventy miles an hour. Through his glasses, he could see a small herd of pronghorns below. The little fellow would feel safer once he was back with the others.

He moved cautiously forward, wondering what had alarmed the antelope. They were jumpy little animals; it might be nothing but the wind. In a min-

ute, he saw two deer, a large buck and a doe. They were a little above him, and there was brush between himself and them. He figured the distance to be about seventy yards. He would have to get the buck with the first arrow; there wouldn't be time for a second one.

Very slowly and carefully, he moved a few feet to avoid the heaviest brush. He fitted the arrow on the leather arrow set, and narrowing his eyes, he sighted through the little cut-out sight window on the handle of the bow directly above his bow hand. He raised his right arm until the bow came up to the level of his eyes, then tilted it a little to the right. Using the corner of his mouth as an anchor point, he pulled the arrow back, aiming at a point slightly above the target. He had stopped thinking of the buck as a living creature; he was intent on his target. He released the arrow, holding the position while he listened to the slight whoosh it made. The buck, catching the sound, lifted his head, but he moved too late. The broadhead arrow sliced into his chest cavity. He lunged, fell heavily, and lay still. The doe had already leaped out of sight.

His hand trembling, Jamie put down the bow and climbed up to the dead buck. He couldn't let himself think about how the buck had looked standing there in the grass with its head up. Instead, he had to dress it out. It was a job he hated, but he was used to it; he had had to help with the butchering of farm animals all his life. From the beginning of his hunting, Pa had insisted that he dress out his game himself and not let Ted do it for him.

He pulled some rocks over to the carcass and placed them at the left hip and shoulder so he could roll it over on its back, with the animal's head uphill. He unsheathed his knife and went to work, his mouth set in a tight line. It was a bigger buck than the one Ted got last year, he decided, and immediately was ashamed of having thought it. Well, Pa would be pleased; it was a lot of meat.

To keep his mind off what he was doing, he thought about Ma. He hoped she had gone over to Aunt Martha's so she wouldn't be lonesome. She'd be able to use that new recipe for venison pie that the ladies at the church had given her.

He glazed the exposed meat with blood to protect it against the blowflies; and then, leaving the carcass in the sun to dry, he went over to the stream and washed his hands, scrubbing them harder than necessary on the slippery pebbles. For extra protection against blowflies, he got a can of black pepper from his pack and sprinkled it thickly on the meat. He gathered up some deadwood and some big rocks and struggled to get the deer up off the ground. He would have to get Pa to help him bring it in; meanwhile, he could keep it from spoiling.

It was heavy, and he was breathing hard by the time he got it up. He sat down for a few minutes to get his breath and to let the carcass dry out a little more. He sat with his back to it, staring off across the mountains, wondering where the mountain lion was. If he was around, he'd have some of the buck for lunch. But there was nothing Jamie could do to prevent that. By himself, he couldn't hang it. He lay back on the dry yellow grass. He felt terribly tired and depressed. It was always that way when he hunted. He tried to think of something pleasant: Cissy. He must remember to find her a feather. He wondered what she was doing; probably pestering her brother Charlie to take her fishing and getting mad because he wouldn't. Charlie said she sneezed so much she scared off the fish. She did, too, but Jamie sometimes took her along anyway. She was good company.

Wearily, he made himself get up and get the cheesecloth out of his pack. He covered the deer carefully. There were probably coyotes nearby, but they wouldn't come around for twenty-four hours or so till the man-scent had worn off. He made a final adjustment of the rocks under the deer, and for a moment he stood looking down at it. He reached out and touched the forked antler, feeling its hardness, and then he quickly turned away. He slid down to the place where he'd left his bow and started for camp at a fast pace, cutting across open places, not bothering about cover or keeping quiet. The going was steep for a while, and his leg muscles ached. He slowed down a little and then stopped to make sure his direction was right.

After about an hour, he came to familiar signs: the stand of aspen where Ted had gotten the antelope, the clearing where the Columbian ground squirrels had a colony. He stopped for a moment and watched their sentinels, listening to them pipe the alarm. They always reminded him of little fellows in baseball caps standing on tiptoe, shading their eyes against the sun. He laughed and went on.

When he thought he was near enough to camp for Snow to hear him, he whistled. He heard the faint answering yap-yap-yap. He realized, suddenly, that he was very hungry. From the looks of the sun, it was past noon. It would take all afternoon to bring down the buck, so he wouldn't be able to take out after the lion till morning. It was just as well; he was tired, and there was a lot of work still to be done. He hoped the cat wouldn't get clear away.

He caught the smell of wood smoke. Good! Pa was there, and he had a fire going. Food! Jamie broke into a run. All of a sudden, he felt a lot better.

He hallooed and heard Pa's answering shout. Snow came dashing through the brush to meet him, free of the hateful rope. Jamie could smell coffee. Snow leaped toward him, and Jamie caught him in his arms.

"Hi, you big old crazy dog!" He buried his face in Snow's wiry coat. "How've you been? You been lonesome? I missed you." He put him down, and the two ran into the clearing together.

His father was standing beside the fire, poking it with a long stick. He looked up and grinned. Good, Jamie thought; he's had a good morning. He didn't see Darby French, and for a joyful moment, he thought he might have given up and gone home. But then Darby came into sight, prancing like a skittish pony, brandishing a retractable measuring tape, held open.

"Yippee!" he yelled. "What a beauty! Four points. The inside spread is twenty-four inches!" He came up to Jamie and grabbed his arm. "Come and see."

The deer was hung by the antlers from a tree, the carcass spread wide with twelve-inch spreaders, the whole thing wrapped in cheesecloth and sacked in cotton bags.

"Two hundred and fifty, if he's an ounce," Darby said. He was jubilant, his face flushed. "Wait till the fellows in the English department see this!"

"Where'd you get him?" Jamie noted that the rack was not as wide as his buck's. He went back to the fire, Darby crowding behind him.

"Oh, up there in the hills somewhere," Darby said.

"In that little clearing near Canyon Creek," Pa said to Jamie. "Past the gulch where the black bear's den is."

Jamie nodded. "I know where you mean."

Pa handed him a tin plate full of scrambled eggs and bacon. "Any luck?"

"Yeah," Jamie said casually. "I got one."

Darby peered at him. "How big?"

Jamie shrugged. "I don't know."

"Not as big as *that* feller, I imagine," Darby said. Then he laughed. "Don't mind me. I'm just so damned proud of my old buckaroo."

Jamie held out his hand for the cup of coffee his father gave him.

"Far?" Pa asked.

Jamie told him where the buck was.

Pa nodded. "We'll bring him in this afternoon."

Jamie sat down on a log, eating hungrily. The food tasted wonderful. Pa was a good camp cook.

"Man, wait till my wife sees that head," Darby said. "You know a good taxidermist, Clarke? Around

Denver?"

"No, I don't," Pa said.

"I wonder where I can find one."

"Look in the Yellow Pages," Jamie said. Pa shot him a warning look, but Darby took it seriously.

"Good idea, son. I'll do that. That deer was so damned beautiful running across that clearing. I think if I'd missed him, I'd have sat right down and bawled." He pulled a small bottle of acetone from his pocket. "You think I ought to do a little more cleaning on the cape, Clarke?"

"I'd leave it alone," Pa said. "He's good and clean." He held out a plate. "You'd better eat."

"I'm too excited. Well, it does smell good." He took the plate and sat down next to Jamie on the log. "It was the funniest thing," he said to Jamie, "the way your father and I saw the deer at the same time. We both shot at him, almost simultaneously. Bam! bam!" He shoveled a forkful of egg into his mouth. "But lucky for me, my shot got him."

Jamie looked at his father. "How far away from him were you?"

Pa avoided looking at him. "About a hundred and fifty yards, I'd guess."

"Your father missed, but I got him, right in the heart," Darby said. "How's that for a city slicker?"

Jamie was still looking at his father. Pa wasn't the

greatest shot in the world, but Jamie was sure from his face that it was his shot that had brought down the deer. He'd like to see the bullet, Jamie thought. "Was he running, or what?"

"Yes," Darby said. "Just starting. Something spooked him, and he took off with that stiff-legged hop. For a second, all I could see was that white rump patch and that crazy black-tipped tail held down. Then he swerved, and he was a perfect target."

Pa took a can of beans off the fire, using his handkerchief for a potholder, and dished up beans for Jamie and Darby. "Soon as we finish with the grub, we'll go up and bring in Jamie's deer." He looked at Darby. "You don't have to go, though."

"Oh, sure, I'll help out," Darby said.

Not wanting him to go, Jamie said, "Pa and I can bring it in all right."

"Well, if you're sure," Darby said. He gave them a boyish grin. "You guys will have to forgive me if I'm not good for much right now. I'm so damned excited about that buck."

"It isn't your first one, is it?" Jamie asked. He couldn't understand why Darby was so wrought up.

"No, I've gotten one or two back east, but they were little fellers, nothing like this." He shook his head in a kind of dazed disbelief. "This is what I came west for. This is the real thing."

When they had eaten, Jamie and Pa got the horses and set off to bring in Jamie's buck. Jamie was still puzzling over Darby. Why would a grown man carry on that way about killing a deer, especially if he thought it was beautiful?

As if he had read Jamie's mind, Pa said, "Darby's like a kid with his first fish."

"Why is he so excited?"

Pa shrugged. "Buck fever. And nobody gets it worse than a dude."

Jamie moved ahead of Pa to lead the way, and in his concentration, he forgot about Darby. It was a beautiful day. He had left his heavy hunting pants and jacket in camp, and the sun felt good, warming him through his thin jeans and sweat shirt. It was great to be alive.

4

JAMIE RODE SLOWLY OVER THE ROUGH GROUND, PA behind him with one of the packhorses. There was no chance for conversation, but Pa wasn't much for conversation anyway, at least, not with Jamie.

Once, when they came to a clearing, Jamie held back till Pa was abreast of him. "Did Darby really get that buck?" he asked.

"I wouldn't hardly think that was any of your business."

Jamie flushed and touched Candy's ribs with his heels to pull ahead. Pa hadn't sounded cross, but he had squelched him the way you'd squelch a little kid. Children should be seen and not heard, that was what Pa always said. Jamie urged Candy over the rough ground. At the edge of the clearing, she stumbled.

"What are you pushing that horse like that for?" Pa called. "Slow down."

"Yes *sir*," Jamie muttered under his breath. "Ho up, Candy." He knew he was being childish, but he couldn't help it. When people treated you like a baby, you began to act like one. It was plain that Pa had shot the buck. And it was plain that he was letting Darby think it was his because Darby wanted it that way, and Darby was paying. It didn't seem like Pa, though, to be dishonest. One thing about him was that you could rely on what he said. Jamie couldn't figure it out. He knew Pa needed money, but to lie for it!

After about an hour, they stopped by a stream to rest the horses and to eat Spam sandwiches from Pa's pack. "Much further?" Pa asked.

"No."

"You think we can get the horses up there?"

"No. It's too steep. We can get them in close, though."

Pa lay back on the stubbly grass and closed his eyes. In a minute, he was asleep. Jamie let him sleep for about ten minutes, and then he said, "Pa. We'd better get with it."

Instantly, Pa was awake. He went to the stream, soaked his head in the cold water, and came up gasping. "That ought to do 'er." He climbed on his horse and waited while Jamie caught Candy. Jamie mounted up and moved out ahead of Pa.

When they'd gone as far as he thought they could go, he slid out of the saddle and pointed up the mountain to the little meadow where the buck was. "We'll have to climb now."

Pa dismounted and took from his pack the piece of canvas they would use to bring the deer down. Jamie scrambled up the side of the mountain, digging his toes into the loose shale. He knew he was going too fast for Pa, but he was anxious to get up there and see if the buck had been bothered by anything, a mountain lion, for instance. All the way along from the camp he'd kept an eye out for the cat, though he knew it was unlikely that the cat would let them get a look at him, even if he was around. You never could tell, though. Sometimes they didn't seem cautious at all.

He came to the place where he'd made the shot. He looked back at Pa, who was coming up over the incline. "I shot him from here," Jamie said. Pa nodded, not wasting breath on words.

Jamie went on up. The buck was right where he'd left him, and as far as he could tell, nothing had touched him. He knelt down and stroked the black forehead patch. It felt bristly. He sensed Pa standing behind him, but he didn't let himself turn around till Pa spoke.

"It's a nice buck," Pa said. He didn't sound excited about it. Just said it was a nice buck.

"I think it's bigger than the one Ted got last year." The minute he said it, he wished he hadn't. It was childish. Pa gave him an odd look, but he didn't answer. Instead, he got to work moving the carcass onto the canvas so they could get it down to the horses.

The mid-afternoon sun grew warmer in spite of a wind that blew more or less steadily at that elevation. It was hot work getting the buck down the slopes and over the rocky ground. Once, the canvas caught on a sharp boulder that tore a jagged rent in it.

By the time they had loaded the deer onto the packhorse and started back to camp, Jamie was so tired he could hardly sit in the saddle. He was hot and sweaty, and all his muscles ached. He kept falling asleep and jerking awake just in time to keep from sliding off the horse.

When Pa spoke, Jamie came to with a start. "I might take a look around over there in the morning and see if I can find an elk before we leave," Pa said. He was pointing to the area where Jamie had seen the mountain lion.

"I doubt if you'll find much game over there," Jamie said.

"How come? There was elk in there last year."

"I saw a mountain lion in there this morning."

Pa gave him a quick interested look, but he said nothing for a few minutes. "Whereabouts, exactly?" he asked finally.

Jamie described the place.

"I suppose you want to stalk him."

"Yeah." Why he wanted to so much, he didn't know himself. It just seemed like something he had to do, as if he would learn some big secret when he finally saw the lion right up close. "I could come back after we get the meat home, or if you're going to hunt in the morning, I could take a quick look. I'd like to get some pictures."

"We'll see." Pa said no more on the ride back to camp.

Darby looked curiously at Jamie's buck. "Nice," he said. "I think mine's a little bigger, though, don't you?" He smiled at Jamie. "No offense."

"Might be, a little," Pa said.

"You could measure the rack," Jamie said coldly. Pa could see perfectly well that his was bigger than Darby's.

Darby didn't offer to measure it. He stood watching as Pa washed the deer, and Jamie helped him hoist it up into a tree.

"We better keep the horses close in to camp," Pa said.

"Why?" Darby asked.

Jamie held his breath. He knew his father was thinking of the mountain lion, and he didn't want him to tell Darby.

Pa didn't answer for a minute. Then he said, "I like to know where they are."

When the work was done, Jamie unrolled his sleeping bag and went to sleep almost at once. When he awoke, the woods were dark, and Pa had a fire going. Jamie got up, smelling Pa's good mulligatawny stew.

"I been looking at the bucks," Pa said casually. "I do believe that Jamie's buck is a little mite bigger than yours, Darby."

Darby stiffened, and for a moment he didn't answer. Then, as if it was of no importance, he said, "Well, it's hard to say unless you weigh them out."

Jamie was pleased that Pa had spoken the truth about the buck.

Darby lifted his arms. "Look at those stars. Gad, you don't see stars like that in the city. This is the life, all right. This is what man was meant for."

Pa got a bottle of bourbon from his pack. "Let's

drink to a successful day." He poured out generous slugs for Darby and himself into paper cups, and a small amount for Jamie.

"Thanks." Jamie was pleasantly surprised. He'd never had any whiskey handed to him by Pa before. Maybe it was a reward for getting a good big buck. They'd have meat for some time, even if they didn't get anything more.

Pa and Darby sat around the fire drinking bourbon and water after supper, and Jamie lay on his sleeping bag, his fist propping up his cheek, listening sleepily as the men talked. The more Darby had to drink, the more boastful he got about his marksmanship.

"I practice all winter, you know," he said. "I tell you, Clarke, I keep myself ready, and I jog three miles every morning."

Ready for what? Jamie wanted to ask.

"There's a target range I go to when the weather is good, and when it isn't, I practice in the basement of my house."

"You got to watch that," Pa said. "A man can deafen himself."

"I know. I have, to some extent. I'm partly deaf in my left ear." He sounded proud of it. He reached for the bottle and poured a generous slug, not bothering with water that time. "I grew up on Hemingway," he said. "I'd have given an arm and a leg to have known that man. You ever read him, Clarke?"

"No," Pa said.

"Well, I don't suppose you're much of a reader."

Jamie bristled at the condescension. "My brother had all of Hemingway's books," he said. He didn't know if that was true, but Ted had had a couple of them.

"Is that right?" Darby said. "Well, one of these days I'll go on an African safari and bring back a kudu head for my study. Won't that be something! I can afford it now. I came into some money this summer. A rich uncle kicked the bucket."

Jamie couldn't resist asking the question that was on his mind. "Why do you want to kill game?"

Darby looked startled for a moment. "Well, like they say about climbing a mountain—because it's there; it's a challenge. I suppose every man is a hunter at heart. He loves nature, and he wants to conquer it."

"I don't," Jamie said. "I don't think anybody in my family feels that way."

"You take it for granted because you live with it," Darby said. "If it came right down to it, you'd opt for being a conqueror, too. It's human nature."

Jamie started to answer, but his father spoke up.

"We should get some sleep." He got up and began to damp down the fire. "Dawn comes early."

"I'd love to get an elk," Darby said. "Any elk around here, Clarke?"

"Sometimes."

Jamie slid down into his sleeping bag and zipped it up. Snow snuggled up against him. He wanted to think some more about his conversation with Darby, but he was too sleepy. He went to sleep thinking about the big cat.

5

JAMIE WAS AWAKE BEFORE SUNRISE, BUT PA WAS already cooking breakfast. Darby wasn't in sight. Jamie washed the sleep out of his face and checked over his gear. He transferred the things he'd need from his pack to his jacket pockets and then shinnied up a tree and hung the pack, the bow, and the quiver of arrows where they wouldn't be seen from the ground.

"You going to look for elk?" he asked his father.

Pa didn't look up from the frying pan. "No."

"You going home? You want me to help take the meat in? I can come back later by myself." He didn't want to go home; he was all revved up to look for the cat, but he knew he ought to help.

"No," Pa said. "We figured we'd come too."

"With me!" Shocked, Jamie spun around to look at him. "Pa! I'm going to track the mountain lion."

"I know that. Darby thought he'd like to see a big cat. It isn't every day a man sees one of them anymore."

Jamie felt sick. "Pa, please. I can't track the lion with other people tramping along with me. Please, Pa, listen."

"Sure you can. We won't crowd you. You can move a half-mile or so ahead of us. You and that cat of yours won't even know we're there."

"Pa, he's my cat."

"What makes him yours?"

"I'm the one who saw him."

Pa looked up, frowning. "The woods don't belong to you, Jamie. Darby wants to see a cat up close. He wants you to take his picture after you've treed the cat, a picture of him and the big cat."

"I won't do it. I won't go."

Pa's eyes blazed. "Oh, yes, you will. Don't tell me what you will and won't do."

Jamie walked off into the woods and leaned his head on his arm against a tree. He felt betrayed. It wasn't like Pa to do such a thing. He must have had it in mind all along, and that was why he'd brought Snow.

In a minute, his father came up to him. "Jamie.

I'm sorry I blasted off like that. That's not fair to you . . ."

"If you want to be fair to me . . ." Jamie was too upset to be able to finish the sentence. "You planned it all along; you brought Snow just to . . ."

"Listen a minute, will you?" Pa said impatiently. "I'm trying to tell you something."

"All right."

"You know I don't ordinarily hire out as a guide. Haven't done it since I was a young man. Never did like it. I did it this time because I needed the money . . ."

"If you'd let me go to work . . ."

"You may have to go to work, but I need money right now." Pa stopped and took a deep breath. "If I don't come up with my back taxes, we'll lose the place."

Jamie stared at him. "Lose the place? *Our* place?"

"Your mother and I have farmed that place; we built the house with our own hands, raised you boys . . . lived there all our married life. I don't have to tell you, do I, what it would do to your mother, after losing Ted, to lose the place, too. We'd have to move to the city, and I'd have to work for wages—a thing I've never done." His voice shook.

Jamie felt stunned. He couldn't believe it. "How

could that happen? How could they take our place?"

"I just told you. I owe taxes. I've been bled to the bone trying to pay the hospital and the doctors. I've let everything go. If Ted was here to help . . ." He gave a sad little laugh. "But if he was here, we wouldn't have the problem."

"What about a mortgage or something?"

"I'm mortgaged to the hilt."

"Pa, I didn't know . . ."

"I know you didn't. But now I'm telling you. Darby French can save our place for us; it's as simple as that. He's paying me two hundred dollars for the deer hunting; but when I told him about the cat, he offered me another five hundred."

Jamie felt cold in his stomach. "Pa, he'll shoot the cat."

"Of course he won't. I've explained to him it's out of season. He knows all that. The man's not a fool."

"No, but he's excitable. He could lose his head."

"You let me worry about that. You just lead us to the cat."

"I don't know if I can, even."

"You can try. And if you start wanting to chicken out of it, just think of your mother. The money for the deer hunt is a help, but it won't be near enough."

68

Darby called to them. "Where are you guys?"

"Just leave it to me," Pa told Jamie. "You just do your part. I'm counting on you. Understand?"

Jamie nodded. He couldn't trust himself to speak. In a minute, he followed Pa back to the camp fire.

Darby was bouncy with enthusiasm. "Listen, I never thought I'd see a mountain lion! An honest-to-God cougar! I thought they were just about gone."

"There are a few around," Pa said. "Not too many in these parts anymore, and they're hard to find."

"I may not be able to find him," Jamie said. "In fact, I probably won't be able to."

"Oh, you'll find him," Darby said. "Your father says you're a good tracker."

"You can't shoot him, you know. Only in March and April."

"I know. Your father told me. But what I figure is, you get him treed; then, I'll lean up against the tree looking like the great white hunter, and you take some pictures. See?" Darby laughed happily. "I'll have the best one blown up and framed." He slapped his thigh. "Wow! I can see Ethel's face now! Ethel is my wife; she thinks my hunting is a big joke. My Hemingway complex, she calls it. She thinks I'd panic if I ran into a dangerous animal."

"Mountain lions aren't dangerous," Jamie said. "Unless they're rabid or wounded or something."

Darby laughed. "Well, don't tell my wife."

Jamie waited impatiently while they got ready. Once he got on the trail, maybe he could think of some way out of this.

"Let's go," Pa said finally.

"Are we going to use the horses?" Darby asked.

"No. I'd just as leave not get them too close to any cougar."

"Oh, that's why you were concerned about them last night."

"It don't hurt to be cautious."

Jamie started out on the trail at a slow trot.

Darby caught up with him. "Say, boy, when you mount that trophy you've got back there, you'll have to have your girl over to see it. She'll be impressed with the mighty hunter."

"I don't keep trophies," Jamie said.

"Why not? Every boy likes to prove he's a big man."

"We hunt for meat," Jamie said curtly. "We aren't trophy hunters." He pulled ahead of Darby and jumped the stream. Usually, he just waded through it, but right now, he felt like jumping it. He wanted to pull ahead of Darby so he wouldn't have to talk to him.

70

Darby jumped the stream, too. Pa, bringing up the rear, sensibly waded through. "What are you guys trying to prove?" he called to them. "Save your strength."

Pa was right, of course, but Jamie kept on pushing hard, hoping to leave Darby behind. When he got to the open meadow where he had seen the doe the day before, he forgot for the moment about Darby and gave all his attention to looking for signs of the lion. He moved into the brush and climbed more slowly, all his senses alert. Snow made frequent forays into the brush after rock squirrels and pocket gophers. Once he got the lion's scent, he would be all business. When Jamie thought to look back, he saw Pa and Darby about a half-mile behind him, as Pa had promised. He forgot about them again, except for a moment of wondering if Darby could make it up the rock face to the stand of spruce from which he had seen the cat yesterday. It was daylight, but cloudy and cold with frost on the ground. Visibility was poor.

He spent a long time searching the area through the binoculars. He couldn't see anything, but that didn't prove a thing.

When Darby caught up with him, he handed up his gun and then made the climb up the rock fast and recklessly. Jamie had to admit that he was in pretty good condition; maybe he really did jog three miles every day. It sounded like a dumb thing to do, but if you lived in the city, you probably didn't have much choice.

Pa, who had followed at a more leisurely pace, came up over the rock as if it were level ground. The place where you'd see that Pa was a better man than Darby, in spite of his being older, would be when good judgment was needed. Pa wouldn't blow his cool; the fact that he thought Darby would was what worried Jamie.

"Any sign?" Pa asked.

Jamie shook his head. "But when I saw him yesterday, he was heading north. I guess that's the best bet."

"How can you be sure he'd stay on a northerly course?" Darby held out his hand for the binoculars, and Jamie watched him nervously. Darby handled things carelessly, and those were Ted's good six-power binoculars.

"I'm not sure," he said in answer to Darby's question. "But we have to start somewhere. Snow will find out."

"Well, he who hesitates is lost," Pa said. "Let's get movin'."

Jamie held out his hand for the binoculars. "Remember, Snow and I need a half-mile lead."

"What for?" Darby asked.

"Because that's the only way I can do it."

"All right, we'll give it to you," Pa said. "You better blaze a trail, though, for when we lose sight of you."

"Okay." He let himself down to the ledge where the cat had been and then on down to the meadow. He whistled to Snow, who was investigating an old bear den, and showed him the place where the mountain lion had been. At once, Snow caught the scent, cold though it was. He stiffened, sniffed all around the area, looked up at Jamie, and barked.

"Good boy." Jamie patted his head. "Let's go."

Snow started in one direction, came back, started off another way.

"I know," Jamie said. "It's twenty-four hours old."

The dog trotted off at a northwesterly angle across the clearing, stopping once to look back at Jamie. Jamie looked up at his father who, with Darby, was watching from the upper ledge, and then he ran across the stiff rimed grass behind Snow.

On the other side of the meadow, Snow stopped again, investigated various possibilities, then took off along the base of a rocky slope. It was the right kind of country for a mountain lion. Jamie was moving fast to keep up with Snow, and he didn't take the time to look back. Every now and then, he nicked a blaze in one of the western junipers.

After some time, Snow took him away from the slope into a low saddle between two high ridges. It was narrow, and as Jamie moved through it, slipping now and then on the loose shale, he thought, Maybe old Golden Boy has circled back and is watching us from up there somewhere, laughing his head off. Just be careful, lion, be careful. At the end of the saddle, he found evidence that Snow was on the right track. There were scratch signs, easily recognizable, the five- or six-inch depression dug out of the dirt, just the way a domestic cat digs in cat litter. Snow circled it, barking furiously.

Jamie knew that the mountain lion had the habit of continuing on in the same direction he was going, after digging his scratch pile. They went out of the saddle and up a gently rising slope into more juniper. Jamie pulled some of the blue-gray berries off and rolled them between his fingers while he waited for Snow to decide where the trail went.

Snow yipped and took off fast just inside the trees. Jamie saw marks on the straw-colored bark of a lodgepole pine where the cat had stopped to sharpen his claws. It occurred to him that probably the cat still didn't know anyone was on his trail. It made him feel bad; he wished he could tell him not to worry when he found out. I'm not going to let anybody hurt you, Golden Boy—some pictures for me, a thrill for Darby, and cash for Pa. You'll save the farm for Ma and Pa.

Snow slowed down to a steady trot, stopping now and then to make sure he had it right, but never being diverted by anything that came along. Squirrels, birds, a snowshoe rabbit still wearing his brown summer coat, a lumbering porcupine that Jamie almost stepped on—Snow never gave them a glance. Jamie was not surprised not to see any deer, though he saw evidence of their having been there.

Sometimes, Jamie got so absorbed in the trail that he forgot, for a few minutes, to leave any blaze, and once, he backtracked to a turn Snow had taken so Pa would see where they'd gone. The thought came to him that if he really wanted to ditch them, he could just forget the blazing altogether. But he couldn't do it. He felt almost as if he and the lion were both being hunted. He was trapped in a situation that gave him no escape.

Suddenly, Snow stopped. He ran in circles, sniffing. He'd lost the scent. Jamie looked around. They were in a gully, and the sides of the mountain that bordered it were steep and jagged. One side was sheer smooth rock. Part-way up the other, maybe a dozen feet, there was a shelf, and above the shelf,

the ascent was not so steep. Jamie stood still, trying to think what Golden Boy might have done. When Snow's forays in the other available directions turned up nothing, Jamie decided that the cat must have leaped up onto that ledge and perhaps scrambled further up to the place where the ground leveled out in an old game trail that wound around the mountain.

Again, Jamie wished he had the cat's agility and could leap that twelve-foot distance from where he stood. He tied Snow's rope around the dog's chest and, holding on to the other end of it, he looked for a toehold. The one he found was hardly deep enough to hold him, but he decided it was all he had to go on. He studied the handholds above him. He thought he could make it. He put his camera in one of his big pockets, the glasses in the other, and zipped them shut.

He broke off some branches and made an arrow for Pa to see. He smiled grimly, thinking that Darby would have to sweat to get up the cliff. Pa would probably amble on around the base till he found some more reasonable way up, but Darby would try for the spectacular leap just to show that if Jamie did it, so could he.

Jamie got his boot as far into the toehold as he could, gave a spring, and grabbed for the small outcropping he had decided on for a handhold. His canteen banged against his back. With his other hand, he caught a dwarf pine that grew out of a crevice, praying it would hold. Heaving himself up again, he felt his fingers clawing the cold surface of the ledge. With a greater effort, he pulled himself up.

Snow was barking nervously. "All right, all right," Jamie said. He tightened the slack in the rope as the dog scrambled up the rock face. Once Snow missed and swung helplessly in the air, but Jamie reeled in the rope as if he were fishing, and Snow got his paws on the rock again, scrambling and slipping. Jamie leaned back and pulled, and Snow catapulted up over the edge of the rock and landed heavily on Jamie's stomach. Jamie hugged him and laughed.

"Ooof! You knocked the wind out of me."

But Snow had no time for nonsense. He had already found the trail again. Jamie's hunch had been right.

6

SNOW LED HIM OVER ROCKY GROUND AND UP HIGHER into the mountains. The wind was sharp and cold, and the gray sky looked as if there might be snow to come. Last year's hard granular snow was still packed in the depressions at the base of trees and in declivities in the rocks. Jamie put up his hood to protect his ears and neck against the wind, but it cut down his visibility so much that he unzipped it again.

He lost all track of time, and there was no clue in the dark sky. Finally, in a place partly protected by a thicket of low-growing juniper, he called Snow back and sat down for a minute. His face ached with cold, and pains shot up the backs of his legs. He pulled his hood around his ears and sat with his knees pulled up, shivering. He wondered if Pa had kept to his trail all right; sometimes the area had been barren, and there was no way to show how he'd gone except with a pile of stones.

In a minute, he opened his pack and found a box of raisins for himself and a Gainesburger for Snow. The dog seemed tired, but he kept his ears pricked forward, alert, even while he ate.

Jamie didn't rest long. If Pa caught up with him, he might say, "Better call it a day. It's going to snow." Jamie wanted to get it over with. The cat would do his traveling at night, so the closer he could get to him before dark, the better. For all he knew, the cat might be thirty or forty miles ahead of him, but he was counting on the mountain lion's inability to keep up a fast pace.

They came out of the grove into the full force of the biting wind. Jamie settled into a half-walk, half-trot. He had on his archery gloves, but they were not much protection against the cold, and finally he took them off and kept first one hand, then the other, jammed into the fleecy lining of a jacket pocket, flexing and unflexing his fingers to keep the blood circulating. He was afraid to put both hands into his pockets at once in case he lost his footing and started to fall. He knew from the shortness of his breath that they were fairly high.

Snow darted up to the foot of a hogback and stopped, looking up and whining.

"Oh, no," Jamie said. "You've got to be kidding." The hogback rose up, a sheer rock wall with a jagged top, about fifteen feet above him. "If he jumped that, he's even bigger and better than I thought." And there was no way to follow him up there. The wall face was smooth and perpendicular. He started around it, hoping it would offer access on the other side. It didn't.

"What he must have done," Jamie said, "was jump across the chasm from the hogback to that next ledge, and then . . . Oh, gosh, then what?" He felt terribly discouraged. He chewed on some raisins, hoping for a little quick energy. Where would *he* have gone if he were a mountain lion? The cat could have come down off that next ledge, or gone on up higher, or circled back. It would depend on what he had in mind—was he conscious of pursuers and trying to outwit them? Had he been looking for a place to catch forty winks? Had he seen something tasty for supper? Or was he just out for a little Sunday stroll? "If I were a cat," Jamie said to Snow, "I could think like a cat. But I'm not. I wish I was." He remembered, suddenly, that he had forgotten to mark where he had turned off around the base of the hogback. Wearily, he went back to leave some sign.

He nearly jumped out of his skin. For a second, he thought it was the mountain lion standing there under the cliff. But it was Pa in his orange-quilted jacket, his old Navy watch cap pulled right down to his eyes. Darby was behind him.

"Hi," Pa said.

Jamie's voice came out squeaky, like a rusty hinge. "Hi. I just came back . . . I forgot to leave a sign . . ."

"Had a hunch you might have cut around the hogback. Figured when you saw those claw marks . . ." He pointed to a faint scratch near the top of the ledge where the lion's paw had scraped the rock.

Jamie stared up at it. He hadn't even noticed. He must be more tired than he realized; it was a good thing Snow was along to stop him at the right places.

"There's some shelter up ahead," Pa said. "I figure we better quit for the night."

Jamie didn't want to quit. If he had to spend too much time thinking about what he was doing, he wasn't sure he could go through with it. But if he was missing obvious signs like that claw mark . . .

"It's late," Pa said, "and it's fixing to snow. And the dog's tired."

Jamie looked at Darby. He was unusually silent. His beard was frosted, and his nose was red. Jamie felt a small throb of hope. Maybe he'd give up. "All right," he said, "let's bivouac."

They went on to the place Pa had indicated, a semicircle of big boulders that offered protection against the wind. Jamie helped Pa gather up some wood from a deadfall, and in a few minutes, a blazing fire was throwing out warmth. Jamie sat with his back to a heat-reflecting rock, letting his muscles relax from the tensions of cold and fatigue. The fire felt very good. Jamie pulled off his heavy boots and warmed his feet.

"Old Prometheus really did us a favor, didn't he?" Darby said. It was the first thing he'd said. He was crouching close to the fire, rubbing his hands together. His face was losing its pinched look.

"Mr. who?" Pa said. He was slicing up corned beef from a can.

"Prometheus. The god who told man the secret of fire."

"Yeah, yeah," Pa said in the tone Jamie both feared and secretly admired because it revealed Pa's mockery without sounding rude or mean. "We thank you kindly, Mr. what's-your-name."

"Prometheus," Darby repeated, as if he were speaking to a student. He rummaged through his pack for a bottle of bourbon, took off the cap and held it to his mouth, taking long gulps. "Ahhh!" he said. "Nectar of the gods." He handed it to Pa, who took a quick drink and gave it back. "You, son?"

"He better have a bite to eat first," Pa said.

Jamie had intended to say that himself; he wished Pa had let him. But it wasn't really all that important. "Later, thank you," he said to Darby.

He ate hungrily, and before it was dark, he was asleep, curled up near the fire, protected from the cold by the "space blanket" that he carried in his jacket pocket.

When he awoke, it was dark, and Darby and Pa were still sitting by the fire, drinking and talking. Jamie listened to them sleepily. Pa was telling about a Colorado cat somebody had got one time up at Jug Gulch, near Loveland, that weighed a hundred and sixty-four pounds. I'll bet Golden Boy can beat that, Jamie thought.

"Biggest one I ever heard tell of," Pa went on, "was killed by Teddy Roosevelt, somewheres around Meeker. They say it was ninety-six inches long, weighed two hundred twenty-seven pounds."

"Wow!" Darby said. "I'd like to get one of those." He paused to light his pipe. "You know, some of the Mexicans revered the lion as the emblem of their nation. The Miztecus, in the sixteenth century, thought he was sacred—so did the Incas. Even now, in New Mexico, you can find prehistoric puma shrines."

"Indians were great for worshiping wild animals," Pa said. "Well, who knows? Maybe they weren't so far wrong."

The wind had cleared the sky of clouds for the moment, and close above Jamie's head, almost close enough to touch, it seemed, the stars sparkled in the soft black sky. Jamie went to sleep and dreamed that his mountain lion turned out to be the god of the sun.

7

JAMIE SLEPT UNEASILY. SEVERAL TIMES HE AWOKE and shifted his position from one side to the other to warm the parts of him that were not exposed to the fire. Twice, he saw Pa putting more wood on the fire and making instant coffee, and once Darby was up, too, the two of them talking quietly. He wondered if they were talking about the lion.

It was still dark when he awoke to find snow on his face. Light feathery flakes were drifting down, and the wind had stopped. He sat up, wondering what time it was. Pa came up behind him with some wood.

"Morning."

"Morning, Pa. Is it morning?"

"Getting close." He bent over and put some wood

on the fire. Beyond the leaping flames, Jamie saw Darby sit up and stretch.

"What time is it, Clarke?"

"Pushing six-thirty."

Darby got up and flexed his stiff knees. "Time to get the show on the road."

"Maybe we better talk this over," Pa said.

Jamie held his breath. Was Pa going to say better give up the hunt? Maybe the weather would give them an honorable way out; Darby would have to pay *something* after they'd brought him so far, and Jamie would be off the hook.

"What's on your mind?" Darby asked.

"Wondering about the weather." Pa looked at Jamie, and although he didn't ask his opinion, Jamie gave it.

"It doesn't look too good. It's cold and snowing, and we haven't had a real clue for a long time. We haven't got any climbing equipment or ice gear, and not much food. Maybe we ought to call it off."

"I was thinking that," Pa said.

Disappointed, Darby resorted to scorn. "Why, Clarke, I'm surprised at you. I never thought you'd be the man to say quit."

"Sometimes it's good sense."

"From what Seth said, I thought you were a real gung-ho hunter."

Pa shrugged. "Whatever that means." He turned toward the fire. "You want coffee?" He held it out to Darby. "One thing I'm not—I'm not a fool."

"Listen, I have a feeling we'll catch up with the cat this morning," Darby said.

"Never had much faith in feelings," Pa said.

"Look at your dog. He's anxious to go. He's on the trail, all right."

"Snow is cold. He wants to get moving, is all."

Darby bent down to look into Pa's face as Pa poked at the fire. "I'll double the ante, man. Double it! Here, I'll put it in writing." He pulled a small pad of paper and a pen from his pocket, wrote quickly, tore off the page, and gave it to Pa, who put it in his pocket without looking at it.

"It's tempting, Darby. I won't deny it. I need the money bad. But the money wouldn't mean much if one of us was to slip and get hurt or killed—or lost in the storm."

"But a man with your knowledge of the mountains . . ."

Jamie could tell that Darby's needling was making Pa mad.

"It's my knowledge I'm talking about. If we go much higher, there's precious little shelter. Not much in the way of small game for food either, and whatever there is will likely stay put while it's storming. There's long stretches up there with no fuel."

"I thought a real mountaineer could make it any time, anyplace."

"Well, you thought wrong." Pa's voice was tight. "My oldest boy was the best mountaineer I ever knew, and the mountain killed him."

Darby was silent for a moment. "I'm sorry. I didn't know that. I'm really sorry." He drank his coffee, looking off at the peaks that loomed faintly white in the falling snow. It was hard to tell where the mountains left off and space began.

Jamie couldn't sort out his own feelings. He felt a great relief at the thought that they might not go after the lion and, at the same time, bitter disappointment. For some crazy reason, that particular mountain lion had come to mean something special to him. He might never have another chance to catch up with it. Like Darby, he felt that the lion was near, and he knew Snow felt it. The dog kept darting off and coming back to whine at Jamie. If he could find the lion, take pictures, and clear out before they caught up with him, Jamie thought, he could say the cat got away. Then he could take a picture of Darby out in the woods somewhere and superimpose the picture on the one with the cat. His wife would probably never know the difference.

89

"Tell you what," Darby said. "Jamie and I will go out for a half-hour, and if the dog doesn't pick up the trail in that time, we'll meet you here."

"No," Jamie said quickly. "No, that wouldn't work."

"Why not?" Darby was getting exasperated. "Why do you think nobody but you can track that damned cat?"

"If I do it, I have to do it alone, that's all."

"What's so great about tracking a cat? If you've got a good dog, anybody can do it." He threw part of his coffee into the snow.

"Take it easy," Pa said. "And don't waste that coffee, we haven't got much."

"I'm sorry," Darby said. "But I'm nerved up. I'm ready to go, Clarke, and we stand here wasting time. If you're worrying about the horses and the meat, as you said last night, why not send the boy back and let him take care of them? You and I can track the cat."

Pa shoved his wool cap onto the back of his head. His eyebrows were white with frost. "Darby, you and I wouldn't come within a hundred miles of that cat. I'm near-sighted. You're inexperienced. The boy and the dog are a team, my oldest boy trained them. If anybody can do it, they can." He turned away. "I want to think about it a little bit." He walked over to a little rise and stared off at the mountains.

"It's your brother he's thinking about," Darby said. "He's scared something will happen to you."

"My father is not scared of anything." As he heard himself say it, Jamie was reminded of the times he'd said that when he was a little boy. "My pa's not scared of anything. My pa can beat your pa."

"Where'd your brother get killed, anyway?" When Jamie didn't answer, Darby asked the question again.

"Long's Peak."

"Long's Peak! Good God! What was he doing up there? Nobody but an expert belongs on Long's Peak."

"He *was* an expert."

Darby shook his head. "Crazy kids."

Jamie looked at him; Darby was jogging in place by the fire, his beard frozen solid and jutting out from his pale chin. He had taken off his glasses because of the snow, and his eyes were watering. Jamie felt a surge of real hatred for him. The man didn't belong there; he was an intruder, a destroyer. And what was he, Jamie, doing helping him? Nothing was worth that. But then, he thought of Ma losing her home, Ted's room gone to some stranger, the tack room not theirs any more, all the stock sold, and Pa, renting a place somewhere, working for wages.

His father turned toward him. "Jamie, come here a minute."

He went over to where his father stood.

Pa pointed off to the east where a thin streak of light showed behind the mountain peaks. "Looks like she's going to clear. Maybe it's a sign." He gave Jamie a small grin. Ma was always saying things were a sign. "If the cat's anywhere near, tracking will be easy with the snow on the ground. We'll give it till noon. If you don't find anything to go on by then, you turn back, you understand? I don't want to risk another storm, and I don't want your mother to start worrying."

"You and Darby go back, Pa. Let me go alone. I'll get the pictures for him." When his father looked at him without answering, he said, "I don't trust him. He'll do something dumb."

"I'll do the worrying about him."

"Then stall him, Pa. Give me a chance to get there."

His father studied him. "You're acting real silly about that cat. What are you planning to do, hold some kind of lodge meeting with him? He's just another varmint, Jamie."

Jamie didn't know what to say. There was no way to explain what the cat meant to him without sounding crazy. "I just wish you'd keep him back."

"The man wants to see the cat for himself. Wants you to get a picture of him standing near the cat. Don't ask me why. I quit trying to figure people out thirty years ago. All I know is, I gave the man my word. Barring it gets too dangerous, if you can tree the cat, he gets to see him. That's the agreement." Pa turned back to the fire and said to Darby, "The boy's going. We'll follow in fifteen minutes."

Darby gave Jamie his most winning smile. "Thanks, Jamie. I appreciate it."

As soon as they were out of sight of the camp, Jamie said, "All right, Snow, take off fast. Find that scent and let's go."

He had been afraid Snow would have trouble finding the trail, but the dog circled around to the far side of the hogback, yipped, and went off at a fast run. Pleased, Jamie trotted after him, slipping now and then on the new snow. He made himself slow down a little. He wanted to get as big a lead as he could, but it wouldn't do to fall on the slippery ground and sprain an ankle or something.

The snowfall grew lighter and finally stopped altogether. Pa's sign had been right. The sky was a pale gray, and the wind stopped howling. If the cat was moving up ahead of them—not too far—it would be possible to pick up his tracks in the snow any time.

After another half-hour or so, he heard Snow yipping his high excited yip, and he broke into a run, sliding on loose shale, falling, picking himself up, and running again. Snow was dashing back and forth, quivering all over with excitement. Jamie ran up to him, and there in the snow, at the foot of a five-foot slope, were the cat's prints. Jamie clapped his hand over his mouth to keep from yelling with delight. The prints were recent. From there on, they would have to move with extra caution. He quieted Snow, holding him still. "All right," he said. "From now on, take it cool." He released the dog and watched him go.

Jamie followed the prints in the protective cover of the trees that edged open ground. It was level, and he could move fast. He felt better, and he kept having the notion that Ted was with him and Ted would make it come out okay. He must be losing his mind, he thought finally; it was the altitude. But in spite of the itchy worry about Darby, he felt good. Pa had said he'd do the worrying about Darby, so let Pa handle it.

8

FOR A LONG TIME, JAMIE FOLLOWED SNOW. SOME-
times, where the wind had blown the ground clear,
there were no prints, but the dog stayed steadily on
the scent. The sun was up, but it was very pale in
the hazy sky, like a slice of one of those oranges
they got sometimes in the winter that were kind of
white and dry. The wind was strong again on the
back of Jamie's neck, but that was okay, too. It
meant the lion wouldn't catch his scent. He ate his
last box of raisins as he hiked along and stopped at
a plunging little waterfall to refill his canteen. He
didn't feel tired at all; he seemed to have gotten his
second wind, and he felt as if he could go forever.
The muscles in his legs didn't hurt anymore. Even
the altitude had stopped bothering him. And some-

how, Darby didn't seem real.

Snow took him up along a watershed for quite a distance. Below them, he could see a silvery streak of upland river cascading off to the east. Then the trail led up to a small pleateau.

Snow stopped on the edge of the plateau where the land sloped steeply down about thirty feet. It was an incline he could slide down—if he was careful—but Snow's hesitation told Jamie the lion had jumped. He lay on his stomach and looked down at the snow-covered ground below him. With his binoculars, he could see the indentations made in the snow by the cat's soft footpads. The tracks veered off to the west where thick brush four or five feet high bordered an open area. At the far end of the long narrow clearing, he saw three white-tailed deer grazing in a place where the wind had blown the snow off.

So that was it! The lion was looking for food. Jamie moved the glasses slowly around the edge of the clearing, searching for the cat. He couldn't see him. Snow was nervous.

"Sit, boy," he commanded him. "Sit. Be quiet. Stay." He put his hand on the dog's muzzle and held it for a moment. Then he looked through the glasses again. He lay very still for ten or fifteen minutes, trying to find the cat. He knew he was

there, somewhere. The sun had burned off most of the haze, and the image of the meadow grew sharper in his glasses. The wind was steady from the south, but not as strong or as cold as it had been. It was pleasant lying there on the ground with the stir of excitement growing in him as he looked for the cat. He thought of the mountain lion Ted had seen once through those same binoculars, playing with a big grasshopper the way Daisy played with a mouse—batting it with his big paws, pretending to pounce, rolling over like a kitten. It must have been a yearling, Ted had said, still young enough to enjoy a good game.

He tensed. He swept the glasses slowly again over a clump of dwarfed wind-bent spruce. He thought he'd seen something . . . He had! It was the lion.

The cat was stalking the deer, slinking along on his belly so slowly that he hardly seemed to move at all. The only motion Jamie could really see was the constant lashing of the long dark-tipped tail. The chin of the small beautifully shaped head seemed almost to be resting on the ground; the big rounded ears pricked forward. Fascinated, Jamie watched the infinitely slow progress toward the unsuspecting deer, who were about thirty or forty yards away. The wind was in the cat's favor, just as it was in Jamie's.

Keeping one arm around Snow, Jamie lay still, losing all track of time. It was as if time had gone into another dimension or had stopped existing altogether. He forgot about his father and Darby, about everything except the big cat inching forward like doom, the three deer, and a hawk that circled lazily overhead, waiting to pick up a meal when the cat was finished.

He didn't know how close the lion would have to get before he jumped, but he thought it would be pretty close. The lion had to rely on surprise and strength; he was no match for a deer in speed. He remembered his biology teacher saying that deer had had to develop their grace and speed to save themselves from their predators.

Although he could have sworn that, at least part of the time, the cat wasn't even moving, he had actually covered some distance since Jamie started watching him. Pretty soon . . . one of the white-tailed bucks lifted his head, and Jamie held his breath. The lion's keen eyes saw the movement, too, and he froze. Then the deer moved away a little from the other two, nearer the lion, and began to graze again. After a moment, the lion resumed his creeping approach. The tension increased. Jamie could feel the palms of his hands sweating, and he

99

kept forgetting to breathe.

The lion was close to the deer, maybe forty feet; the tip of his tail twitched furiously. He moved a little closer, and then, as Jamie watched, he drew his feet under his body and tensed his muscles. There was a long moment when nothing happened, and then, the lion sprang at the deer. First, he was just yellow smoke sailing through the air, and then he was a writhing mass of muscles as his claws tore into the fallen deer's back, and his teeth gripped the neck. In seconds, before Jamie could even sort out what was happening, the deer was dead.

Jamie was trembling, as Ma would say, "like a leaf," and he had to move the glasses away from his eyes for a moment to wipe the sweat from his forehead. When he focused on the animals again, the lion had rolled the carcass of the deer on its back—its legs sticking up in the air—and with his teeth in its brisket, he was dragging it out of the open field to shelter. The other deer had disappeared. The hawk swooped a little lower to have a look.

When the lion got the carcass where he wanted it in the concealing brush, Jamie couldn't see it any more. All he could see was occasional motion in the brush, and once, the cat's powerful shoulder as he moved around the deer.

Jamie felt exhausted, as if he himself had made

the long tense stalk. He put his glasses down and leaned his head on his arms.

"Jamie."

He started up. He couldn't believe that he had fallen asleep. What a time to sleep! And now, here were Pa and Darby, looking tired and cross. His stomach tightened.

"We lost your trail," Pa said. "Had one hell of a time finding you."

"I'm sorry." Jamie wanted to take a quick look to see if the lion was still there, but he didn't. He held the binoculars loosely in his hand.

Pa was examining the meadow with his own glasses.

"Well?" Darby asked impatiently. "Did you see him?"

Jamie wanted to say no, but he couldn't lie with Pa standing there. "Saw him at a distance," he said, trying to sound casual.

"Where? How close?"

Pa pointed to the place in the open grass where the lion had jumped the deer. "Looks like a ruckus went on down there." He looked at Jamie. "Did he jump a deer?"

Jamie nodded. Without looking directly at the place where the cat had dragged the deer, he tried to squint his eyes and see if there was any sign of his still being there. He couldn't see anything. The hawk wasn't in sight either. How long had he been asleep? Maybe the cat had eaten what he wanted, buried the carcass, and moved on.

"Well, what are you doing up here?" Darby demanded. "Why aren't you after him?" His voice was loud and excited.

"Not too smart to monkey with an animal that's feeding," Pa said. "Especially when there's no tree to climb."

"He may be down there right now. What are we waiting for?"

"If he *was* there," Jamie said, "he'd be gone by now; he'd have heard you."

Darby flushed. "Look, you're the great tracker. Find him. Man, if we're this close . . ."

"Don't push the boy," Pa said to Darby. "Give him his head."

"Let me take a look." Darby grabbed the binoculars out of Jamie's hand so unexpectedly that the strap caught on Jamie's wrist.

"Watch out!" Jamie made a grab as the strap jerked loose, but it was too late. The glasses flew out of Darby's hand and fell down the slope, bouncing off rocks. Jamie heard the glass splinter.

"Damn it!" He glared at Darby.

"I'm sorry. I'll buy you some new ones."

"Those were my brother's glasses."

"I said I'm sorry. Just let me know what kind, and I'll replace them." Darby turned to Pa. "I'll get him some new ones, for God's sake."

"Better get going, Jamie." Pa's face was set in tight lines.

He had to get out of there, Jamie knew. He gave Snow a little push. "Go, boy." He stepped over the edge of the cliff and started down, going faster and faster as his momentum carried him, going in a reckless way that ordinarily he would have scorned. He dug in his heels and slid, trying to keep his balance. About six feet from the bottom, he jumped. It was a stupid idiotic thing to do; he could have broken an ankle. He fell on the hard ground, scooped up the broken binoculars, jammed them in his pocket, and took off across the clearing in a hard run. He heard Pa call him, but he didn't look back.

Snow disappeared into the brush, following the path the cat had taken when he was stalking the deer. Jamie deliberately overshot the place where he knew the carcass was and plunged into the bushes. Crouching a little, he circled back to the spot where he had last seen the cat. He didn't think Pa could see much with those old field glasses of his, but he kept low, just in case. He wanted as long a head start as he could get.

Snow was there already, nervously whining and poking at the partly eaten carcass. The cat had heaped brush on it before he left, so he must have gone before Pa and Darby showed up; if he had been there to hear Darby's loud voice, he wouldn't have stopped to conceal the deer. Jamie glanced quickly at the carcass; it was an old buck. He'd heard that both wolves and mountain lions usually picked out the old and sick deer; the old and sick were easier to get. It kept the herd strong.

Snow, worrying around the area, picked up the cat's trail and took off, yipping. Jamie followed him, and wherever the ground was clear enough, he ran. It was now or never, not only for catching up with the cat, but for making sure he outran Darby. He wanted time to see the cat by himself and to take his picture. Then he'd get Darby in and out real fast. If he could quit the whole thing, he would do it, much as he wanted to see the cat up close. But he would never be able to get Snow off the trail now. And he kept remembering Pa's voice when he talked about losing the place. What a fix to be in.

He settled into an easy rhythmic run, Snow far ahead of him and out of sight, but giving voice all the time. The trail was heading down, and Jamie knew the cat was heading for bigger timber where he could find himself a good tree if he had to. The sun was really out now, and the snow was melting. For the time being, he stopped worrying about Darby. He knew he was setting a pace Pa couldn't keep up with, and he doubted if Darby could either. He hoped Darby would use some sense about that gun; he handled it carelessly, and Jamie could imagine his tripping or something and the darned thing going off. Just so Pa kept out of the way of it. It was funny—Darby was nervous, and the mountain lion was nervous—but what a difference in the meaning of the word. Darby seemed to be about to come apart at the seams all the time, but the cat was perfectly controlled.

Trotting along the game trail that wound around the face of the mountain, Jamie searched his pockets, hoping to find something left that he could eat. He was hungrier than he could ever remember being. His fingers closed on a thin sliver of jerky and he ate it slowly, making it last as long as he could.

He came around a switchback and found Snow. "What's the matter? How could you lose him?" Snow ran back and forth near the place where the trail had apparently stopped. On their left, the ground fell off sharply in a long drop to the spot below them where the trail wound back and down again. It was too long a drop for the cat to have taken. On their right, the mountain sloped upward gradually with a thick sprinkling of trees.

Snow scrambled up the bank but couldn't find the scent.

"Well, he had to go somewhere," Jamie said. "He didn't just vanish into air." He stood still a minute, studying the ground. The snow here had already melted, so there were no easy prints to follow. He got down on his knees and examined the ground. "He must have pulled the old fox trick," he said to Snow. "There's no other answer. He must have doubled back on his tracks and jumped aside, I'll bet you." He turned around and started back. "Smart feller!" It amused him that the cat had outwitted him. He felt proud of him. How could anybody outsmart a cat like that?

He kept his eye on the ground just above them, trying to see any place that looked as if the cat might have leaped into it from the trail. He couldn't have doubled back too far; there wouldn't have been time.

"There!" A chokecherry tree was broken down, and it looked like a recent break. "Up, Snow." He boosted the dog up onto the higher ground and pulled himself up after him. Snow sniffed around for a few seconds and then began to bark. Jamie laughed. He and the lion were playing a game, and he'd just won a move.

Snow took off at a diagonal through the woods, barking furiously. For a second, Jamie wondered if Pa had been able to keep on the trail. If he had, that doubling trick would save Pa some time. And with all the racket Snow was making, they'd hear him. Come on, old cat, give up! Let me say hello and get those pictures. Then you won't be pestered any more.

The dog's barking took on a new note, high and excited. Jamie broke into a run.

9

FOLLOWING THE SOUND OF SNOW'S BARKING, JAMIE climbed a short steep thickly wooded bank. Off to his right, the land dropped into a narrow gulch a long way down. Jamie came to the top of the bank, where the trees were taller and more sparse. Snow was barking and yipping furiously at the foot of a big spruce.

Cautiously, holding his breath, Jamie moved toward the tree. At first, he couldn't see the cat, but then, as he moved a little to one side, he saw him. The big tawny animal was stretched out on a limb about twelve feet off the ground, his head turned a little so he could keep his eyes on Jamie.

"Well, hello!" Jamie said softly. "I'm glad to see you." The cat was bigger than he'd thought. His eyes, outlined with black, were amber—the pupils just slits in the morning light—and he seemed to be studying Jamie. "Mr. Mountain Lion," Jamie said, "old Golden Boy. Mr. Puma, Cougar, Catamount, Panther, Painter, and all your other names. You are magnificent, you really are." He called Snow over to him. The dog came reluctantly, growling in his throat. "Your job's done, Snow. You did fine."

Moving slowly so as not to frighten the cat, he got his camera out of the case and looked through the finder. The lion's expression interested him. He looked . . . well, thoughtful was the word that came to Jamie's mind . . . as if he were a little perplexed, a little concerned, but not really frightened and definitely not angry. He'd heard you could make a pet of a mountain lion if you got him young. But that would be a crime.

"Smile, King of the Mountain," he said, and clicked the camera. He moved a little way around the tree for a different angle. The cat moved his head slowly, keeping his eyes on him all the time. It was a beautiful specimen—his inch-long coat healthy and clean, his eyes clear. Jamie sighted through the finder. "Hey, that's a good one. I'm sorry I chased you, King. If we worried you any, I'm real sorry. I'll never do this again." He took another picture. "Darby French has had his chance, and he didn't show up. And I'm glad of it. A guy like Darby French shouldn't get anywhere near the king, right? So Snow and I are going now, and you hightail it out of here. I'll tell Mr. French you had another appointment and couldn't wait." He leaned down and slipped the rope through Snow's collar. The dog was still growling deep in his throat. "Quiet, Snow. The show's over."

He straightened up for a last look at the lion. The cat seemed relaxed, though Jamie knew how quickly those great muscles could tense into action. The cat's head was on one side.

"You look kind of dreamy," Jamie said. "What are you dreaming about? Tell me, so I can dream the same thing." He took a long breath, hating to go. This was a moment he would remember all his life, and he wanted to have every detail clear in his head.

The cat made a small quick turn of the head, looking past Jamie. Jamie looked around. He could see nothing. But while he looked, Pa and Darby came up over the incline. Jamie felt the cold fear in the pit of his stomach.

"We heard the dog," Darby said. "Did you find him?"

Pa saw the cat first and stopped in his tracks.

He put out a hand to stop Darby.

"What's the matter?" Then Darby saw him, too. "Great God!" he said softly. "It's him!" For a long moment, he just stared at him, his face gleaming with excitement. "Jesus, he's beautiful! Look how *big!*"

"I've got some pictures," Jamie said. "We'd better get out of here now."

But Darby didn't hear him. He took a cautious step toward the tree, stepping over a rock.

"Watch it, Darby," Pa said softly.

"I'll get your picture, Mr. French." Jamie held up the camera.

The cat was watching Darby, and he didn't seem relaxed anymore. The tip of his tail twitched a little, and the amber eyes were bright. Darby walked a little way around the tree, staring up at the cat as if he were seeing a vision.

"Jamie's got your picture," Pa said. "Better go now, Darby."

"God," Darby said, "look at him, Clarke. He's fantastic. I mean I never saw anything so . . ." He let out his breath. ". . . so beautiful." He moved back again to where he had been standing. "Nobody would believe it . . ."

Without warning, he raised his gun and fired.

Jamie's yell was lost in the roar of the gun, and

already, the lion was falling, blood spurting from his shoulder. Darby stepped back.

The cat hit the ground hard and staggered to his feet, growling. He swayed, turning his head back and forth. Snow was barking.

Jamie turned his face toward Darby with such fury that Darby took a step backward. "I had to," he said. "He's so magnificent."

The cat faced him and snarled. Darby's expression changed to fear. "Clarke . . ." He started to raise his gun again, but once more the lion snarled, a thin cutting sound. Darby jumped back, tripped over a rock, and fell, his gun flying out of his hand. He scrambled to his feet and ran down the hill.

Snow was pulling at the rope, barking wildly. Jamie slapped him, hardly knowing he did it. The lion turned toward Jamie, biting angrily at his wound, his head lowered. His eyes were glazed with pain and rage.

Jamie heard Pa say, "Jamie . . ." The lion was growling. Jamie stood like stone. The lion gathered his feet under him, swaying unsteadily.

Jamie heard Pa's gun blast and saw the lion jolt backward, fall, and lie still, his eyes open. Jamie was unable to move; he felt as if he himself had been torn apart by the bullets. He saw Pa move in cautiously

and look at the lion. "He's dead," Pa said.

The sound of his father's voice released him. Jamie jumped across the body of the cat and grabbed his father by the shoulders, pinning him against the tree. "You killed him."

Pa made no attempt to pull away. "I had to. He was dying. He might have jumped you."

Jamie shook his father furiously. "I trusted you. You brought that killer up here. You said you . . . You made me trap the lion so that maniac could kill him."

Pa didn't answer when Jamie let go of him. He sagged back against the tree. Jamie looked down at the lion. It was hard to believe he could look so dead when he had just been so alive. He bent down, got his arm under the cat's shoulders, and began to drag him over to the cliff. The lion was very heavy.

"What are you doing?"

"He's not going to hang on that bastard's wall." Jamie got his other arm around the cat's chest. It was hard work pulling him over the rough ground. Pa made a movement toward him, but Jamie said sharply, "Don't touch him!"

It took him several minutes to drag the body to the edge of the cliff. Jamie was sweating, and his new jacket was covered with blood. Tears streaked his face. He looked down into the narrow draw at the base of the cliff. "You'll be better off," he said softly. "I'm sorry. I'm sorry." He pushed the lion's body, and it fell, slowly at first, then faster. It hit against the side of the cliff, and then, it fell onto the rocky bottom of the draw. The birds and the coyotes would get him, but he wouldn't hang on Darby's wall. Jamie wiped the tears from his face with his sleeve, streaking it with blood and dirt. He got to his feet.

"Jamie . . ." His father's voice sounded far away and unfamiliar. "I did wrong. I own up to it. I never should have trusted him, but I did it for the money. I swear to you, I never thought he'd shoot the cat. I never thought that."

"You didn't want to think it," Jamie said.

"I know that."

Jamie turned and looked at his father and saw the haggard face, the old face. My pa can lick any guy in the world. My pa can ride the wildest bronc, bring a boat through the worst storm practically by himself, ride the logs down the roughest river . . . My father is an old and tired man who makes mistakes. He felt sick with loss.

He watched his father take his handkerchief out of his pocket and wet it with water from his canteen. He came up to Jamie and tried to wash the blood off his jacket. His hands shook.

"Don't, Pa." Then, as he saw his father wince, he said more gently, "I'll get it cleaned when we get home."

"Blood is hard to get out," Pa said.

Jamie went over and picked up Darby's gun. From there on out, he couldn't lean on Pa for things any more. He would have to make his own choices. It was a scary idea, but in another way, he liked it. He said, "We'd better go find French. He'll never make it back to camp by himself."

"Guess you're right. I can do it, though, if you want to go on home." His father's voice sounded more normal.

They started down the slope. For a while, they walked in silence, Jamie leading the way. On the game trail, Pa caught up with him. "Ma will be pleased with that big buck you got. I believe it's bigger than the one Ted got last year."

"I don't believe so. I think they'll weigh out about the same. But Pa . . ." He hesitated, "It doesn't make any difference. I mean, Ted's gone, Pa."

After a moment, his father said, "You're right. It's hard to say it, though. I miss him."

"Me, too."

In a few minutes, he pointed to Darby's boot

prints. "Guess he won't be too hard to find."

"No."

"Be sure he pays you, Pa."

"Don't worry."

As they came around a curve, Pa leaned down and picked up a long brown feather tipped with gold. "Looks like a golden eagle."

"Cissy will like that."

Pa gave it to him, and he put it carefully in his pocket.

"She'll give you a big hug for that, Pa."

Pa put his hand on Jamie's shoulder for a moment. "I bet she will."